THE HOLLOW MAN

By
Richard Dokey

Paul J. Strassberger
DELTA-WEST PUBLISHING, INC.

Delta-West Publishing, Inc.
2720 Wrondel Way
Reno, Nevada 89502

Manufactured in the United States of America
First Printing: April 1999

Library of Congress Card Catalog Number 94-073943

Dokey, Richard, 1933-
  The Hollow Man
  Richard Dokey
  p. cm.
  ISBN 0-9628923-4-3

I. Title: The Hollow Man

Manufactured in the United States of America
First Printing: April 1999

987654321
First Edition

This book is for Judy Booth Drace

CHAPTER ONE

A figure came out of the trees and was running hard. It was foggy, and with the mist and the street damp and all the cars sweating at the curb, the figure looked as though it were being chased by something in the woods. From the front step of his home, Charlie Bredesen couldn't tell if it was a man or a woman.

Charlie walked to the silver BMW parked in the driveway, opened the door and sat down. He stared at the dashboard, with the deep dark color and the little numbers all painted green. He held the wheel in his hands and a lump came to his throat. "Jesus," he said. "Jesus H. Christ."

He had owned the car already a month and the feeling hadn't worn off. It was like standing at the top of a hill of fresh powder or watching a brown caddis fly curl right in behind a flat rock or seeing for the first time the nipples of someone he had wanted for a while.

He smelled the leather and the polish. It was that new car smell, but it was more than the smell of the Chryslers and Continentals he had tried out. He loved the smell so much that he thought if he could put it into a can so it could be sprayed on anything, he'd make a million. "People need the

1

smell," he said. "They need it like sex."

He backed out of the driveway, and at the moment he had the car parallel to the curb, the runner came by. It was a man, a skinny hermaphrodite with hairy, Buster Keaton legs and bony little arms pumping across a flat chest. The guy stared straight ahead, but the strain was on his placid, immobile face. "Why do the bastards all try to look so cool? I've never seen one of them smile yet. They look like they're sitting on the toilet."

He had recently begun talking to himself and rather enjoyed listening to the sound of his voice in the warm interior of the car, with the windows up and the stereo off and everything new and fresh and him feeling just fine, thank you.

Only this morning Marian had glanced over the newspaper and exclaimed, "Oh, for chrissake, they've gone and burned a cross in some black woman's lawn." She waited a bit, but he didn't say anything. "Charlie, did you hear me?"

"Yes," he said.

"Say, are you feeling all right?"

"I'm feeling just fine."

"You do look a bit lumpy under the eyes."

"Lumpy? What do you mean, lumpy?" He put down the hot croissant, over which he had spread a generous portion of orange marmalade, and stared at the woman upon whose body he had spent so much of his life. "Just because I don't answer you?"

"Don't snap," she said.

He got up and went to the mirror above the chest that contained the china which had come down in her family for three generations and which, naturally, they never used.

He didn't see puffs. There were lines, maybe, as though the eyes had just come out of the dryer and needed pressing, but no puffs.

2

He studied himself a moment and tried to recall just when he had started taking an interest in how his face was put together. Until recently, all action in that area had been motivated by snipping hairs from his nose, applying styptic pencil to a razor cut, inspecting his nostril wings for blackheads or plucking the space between his heavy brows. It seemed to him now, however, that something subtle was going on that he hadn't noticed before. There was something happening there inside his face.

He came back and sat down.

"I'm all right."

"I didn't say you weren't. But don't forget that checkup."

"Checkup?" he replied. "Checkup?"

"Can you imagine Ku Klux Klan shit right here in town?"

Charlie sat in reverse, watching the man run away from him up the street, his red shorts like oversize bloomers flapping about his knobbly legs.

The purr of the engine was the murmur of surf at St. Thomas late at night when everyone was asleep and you had the whole beach to yourself. The feel of the seats was a bed you had never been in before with someone you had only just met. The shine of the leather manufactured visions of saddles and the talk of men with beards high up in the Sierra and no women at night around the campfire.

A longing filled his heart at the very moment he put the car in drive. It seemed to be compressed into the center of all the joy and satisfaction of ownership, like the core of a golf ball when he struck it just right. It was the release of this core that made the ball fly down the fairway, yet in the center nothing was changed, nothing was fulfilled, and there it was at rest in the mown grass waiting to be struck again because it had not yet gone anywhere.

The man running ahead of him produced a sense of effrontery in Charlie. Had the fool come by at just this

3

moment to make him feel guilty about driving? Well, he didn't feel guilty about driving, thank you. He felt particularly good about driving.

He held the car at a speed even with the pace of the runner, who was ten yards ahead of him. What was the reward of such activity? A slower heartbeat? A firmer body? The pride of getting up early in the morning before work, rain or shine (he had observed that these idiots had no sense of weather), and pumping off to a designated point a few miles away and back again?

He pulled the BMW alongside the runner. The man didn't turn at once, and as Charlie watched the joints of the hips, from which the legs were flung and retrieved, like the appendages of a circus wheel, he was aware of a hollowness. In the heart of all this motion, where the legs joined the torso, there appeared to be no movement at all. And this vacuity, carried along in a fluid line down the street, was trapped between the flailing arms and pounding feet, somewhere in the center of the pelvis. At that moment Charlie felt the flesh he was sitting on pucker and send tiny waves of anticipation along his spine.

The man turned his head -- he must have been running for miles -- and there was in his face the look of someone who has seen the bottom of a well. The eyes were empty.

Charlie swerved into the far lane. He had missed the turn onto Treat Boulevard and the ramp that led to the freeway and was greeted by the blare of a horn. A red Mercedes came around, and a man dressed in a houndstooth jacket and matching cap raised a bony finger in salute. "Sonofabitch," he saw the man's mouth say.

He sped up and made a U-turn at the next intersection. When he got back to Treat Boulevard, the runner was gone.

Maybe it was death. Maybe that's what she had wanted him to think about this morning.

4

"And how is Maju?" he had asked over the orange juice. It was the name David had given her mother when he was fourteen months old. Grandma and Juliet. He put them together because he couldn't pronounce them separately.

"She spent a restful night. I called the hospital."

"Well, that's good."

Talking solicitously about her sixty-eight-year-old mother always softened her.

"What do the doctors say now?"

"Oh, you know."

He nodded and watched the kitchen light become fatigued in the corners.

"Well," he said.

Was that a sure sign? Was it all in the organs? Was the very mystery and meaning of existence contained in a carcass of properly functioning bowels, lungs, bladders and glands?

As a kid he had run full tilt into a water faucet planted in the middle of a lawn on a two-foot riser. Took it right in the balls. He had writhed on the ground a minute or two and then had jumped up and finished the game. Now he had to go to a doctor for a permit into life.

Charlie stayed in the right lane all the way to the Caldecott Tunnel. The freeway rose and dipped over the pine-studded hills. In the old days there had been no freeway, just a road going through all the small towns, Clayton, Concord, Pleasant Hill, Walnut Creek, Lafayette, Orinda, where the people lived who couldn't tolerate the effluence of the city. The tunnel was a siphon with a filter of darkness and artificial light that somehow permitted your car radio to work. To the west, between the mountain and the bay, sprawled Oakland and Berkeley, which had gotten even uglier over the years. To the north and south of them, clinging to the edges of the water like debris cast off from passing ships, were the horrid little places, Fremont, Hayward, San

Leandro, Alameda, Albany, Richmond, San Pablo, Pinole.

Charlie liked driving in the right-hand lane of the freeway. He wasn't in a hurry to get anywhere. "Let the bastards go on by. Let them have their three or four extra minutes at the toll plaza." He patted the dashboard.

At that moment one of the BART trains caught up to him. They ran parallel for a time beneath the damp fog. He looked across the lanes of automobiles and saw faces much like his own, hunched over newspapers or staring numbly at the traffic. He didn't enjoy riding BART. It made him feel like something passing down a huge intestine, and when the train moved under the bay, he felt trapped in a dark, gigantic anus.

"They'll have it everywhere one of these days. They'll have it running to Sacramento and Tracy and Stockton. Pretty soon the whole valley will be part of the Bay Area. People are living over there already and working over here. The Chronicle should do a a study about it."

And he tried to recall the days when Mt. Diablo was only a beacon hill for incoming ships and not a hatrack for Montgomery Street.

"It does no good to complain. No goddamn good at all."

He glanced at the green Riviera that had pulled alongside. The woman driver was grinning at him like an ape. Yet she looked oddly familiar.

So what if he talked out loud. "Why do you have to eavesdrop?" There was something evil about one person's peering through shatter-proof glass into the interior of another's automobile. An automobile was like a bedroom, and if a fellow wanted to play with himself there, that was his own damned business, thank you. "Just pretend the shades are drawn and run along, lady."

He stuck out his tongue because now the woman was laughing hysterically.

The Caldecott came upon him all at once, a perfect hole

cut into earth and rock. He gripped the wheel with both hands. The automobiles seemed to float upon a film of oil. The taillights shimmered. The tiled walls gave off a translucent blue flame. The horns sounded hollow and bright, as though they had come across water. Some years before, a gasoline truck had exploded in the tunnel, and a circle of flame had rushed through the entire length, devouring the oxygen. Twenty people suffocated.

Then Charlie understood what Marian had meant. Peering at him across the breakfast table and finding beneath his eyes something that reminded her of poorly whipped mashed potatoes had led her to the deeper reflection that she was a mere six months younger than he and susceptible to the same lumps. He had come in from the bathroom the night before, after having gargled with a liquid that was suspiciously like the color of the blue water in the toilet bowl, and found her pushing at her breasts with a thumb and forefinger.

"What's the matter? Do they need exercise?" he said.

"It's not funny, Charlie. A woman has to watch these things."

"I thought that was a man's job." She still had a swell body.

"I don't like surprises. Would you like to be surprised by something they found inside you later only because you were too afraid to let them have a look?"

She lay flat on her back, her legs apart and the mound of her hair shining in the orange light manufactured by the dimmer. Then she felt under her arms and touched tentatively the sides of her neck. There was something potentially terrible hidden in lymph glands and the fatty tisssue on her chest. That a woman could find such clinical interest about her own tits fascinated him.

"Alison Beltran didn't have a pap smear, and then they

7

found cancer and had to take one off." She finished her inspection and turned her attention to him. "Would you still want me," she asked, "if I had to have breast surgery?"

"Well," he said, standing fully naked before her with not the slightest gesture of desire between his legs -- it must happen like that, he once conjectured, with anyone with whom you regularly have intercourse -- "I'd like both of them off. You know, to sort of balance things."

"I'm being serious, Charlie."

"So am I." But he grinned.

"I just don't want surprises," she said, "when I can do something to prevent them."

"That's wise," he said, lying down beside her.

"Did you gargle?"

There was a ten minute delay at the toll plaza. They jockeyed for position. He stayed put and ultimately they all inched along together.

Many of the cars had three and four people. Riding in a pool made more sense, of course. Every so often they tried to get him into one. He had done it once. Chatter and work gossip and coffee mugs rolling under the seat. How would you like being consumed by a fireball in the Caldecott with three people from the office you could barely tolerate? Not on your life, thank you. If he were going to go, it would be alone, surrounded by glove leather in his personal metal cruiser from the Bavarian Woods.

"I have to work with them all day as it is, for chrissake."

The cars came through the toll gate but had to wait behind a string of lights that controlled the flow of traffic onto the bridge. When it was his turn, he maneuvered to the far right lane and stayed there.

The fog was not so thick as it was across the hills. Something with earth versus water temperature he could never understand. As the car rose toward the Yerba Buena anchorage, he could see the buildings of the financial district emerge, like an armada of tall ships beached upon the shore.

Two thoughts occurred to him, as they almost always did every time he went across the bridge alone. He recalled how at one time he could go to the top of the Fairmont Hotel and have a 360-degree uninterrupted view of the entire city. Now this miniature Manhattan was in the way.

"It's fucked."

That was the other thought.

The traffic moved past the island toward the San Francisco anchorage. It slowed and then stopped.

"Accident," he conjectured.

The cars hobbled along. Five minutes crept by. When he got far enough ahead, he saw that it was a stall, the horror of every commuter.

"Poor asshole."

The car was in Charlie's lane. Gradually the traffic worked forward, peeling off to left and right. He couldn't squeeze out. He came up and stopped. It was the green Riviera.

Charlie waited. The woman's head was against the steering wheel. He could see that she was crying. She was sobbing, for chrissake.

Charlie looked around. The lanes were jammed. People were yelling and swearing.

"Sonofabitch."

Then the door of the Riviera opened and the woman got out. He watched as she stumbled across the lanes and leaned over the railing. This caused the skirt of her red suit to come up above her knees, and he couldn't help noticing she had nice legs. He thought she was being sick, but she gave a little jump and disappeared over the side.

Charlie took his foot off the brake. The BMW went forward, met the bumper of the Riviera, and the engine quit.

People were coming out of their cars, shouting and running. Charlie opened his door. When he got to the railing, everybody was looking down. He looked down too. It made him dizzy. There was nothing to see anyway except water.

CHAPTER TWO

The company for which he worked was considering moving its corporate offices across the bay to San Ramon. That was fine with Charlie. To his way of thinking there was a sort of insular quality about American business. When the Industrial Revolution had shifted the center of commerce to the cities, the American worker had followed, only to become disillusioned at last and flee to something called the suburbs, where there were lawns, trees and barbecue pits.

Now business was following the workers. The rent was cheaper. Parking was easy. There weren't the social and economic problems. And the restaurants weren't half bad.

Still, from the window of his office on the seventeenth floor, Charlie had a good view of the Ferry Building, the docks and the bay on either side of the bridge. He had always enjoyed the view, so much so that long ago he had arranged his desk, chair and filing cabinet so that his back was to the window. He would never get any work done if he could simply lift his eyes and see the sun shimmering on the blue water.

Frank Ruskin always carried on about his view from the north side of the building. "I can see the sunset," he bragged.

So one evening Charlie had stayed late when Frank was in L.A. for a meeting and he went over there and looked out. He could see Angel Island, Sausalito, a piece of Alcatraz and the far edge of the Golden Gate. But he could not see the sunset, not the actual sun setting. It was hidden by other buildings.

Maybe Frank was only suggesting that he could see what happened when the sun went down. Often that's what people meant. "What a beautiful sunset," someone would say, and there would be this strange orange glow between the buildings. What Charlie saw, looking out Frank's window, was that the sky got red, a kind of white translucence covered the bay and all the lights came on in the windows.

Anyway, there was a part of the evening that Charlie could see from his own window that he believed Frank would never appreciate. The long, rectangular shadows creeping across the water. The bridge, a shining, magnificient silver web above the bay. The Berkeley hills lit by the falling sun, like bleachers in a football stadium. The sky over Mt. Diablo going all pink and blue above a purple haze.

But Charlie's window was really a window of mornings. Sometimes in the winter, if the weather was clear, he would leave the house at five and arrive at the office before anyone else got there. Then he would pull the chair over to the window and light a cigarette. The sky was already diluted above the mountains, while on the bridge and all the buildings across the bay the lamps still twinkled, casting glimmering threads across the still water. Then in the east the sky turned faintly yellow and then white, and down by the docks the color of the bay came up out of the darkness. The lamps began going out, and there was a gloss on the windows of the adjacent buildings. Then morning was in the sky and shadows ran down the Berkeley hills, spilling into the bay, and the shining left the water by the docks and hurried over to the Oakland shore.

Charlie had never told Marian the real reason why he left so early on these mornings, and the others at work, seeing the old station wagon parked there when they arrived, made predictions about how far he was going with the firm, and all the while Charlie had only come to see the sunrise.

Now he saw a Coast Guard vessel moving in ever widening circles at a point just below the bridge.

"Poor bitch."

Charlie left the office and walked past his secretary into a large room divided into cubicles. The cubicles were made with five foot white formica slabs, and in them sat people working. Each person had a telephone, an electric typewriter, a computer terminal, ledgers and directories and had personalized the space with glass jars of jelly beans, photographs of unsmiling children, colored boxes of facial tissue, coffee mugs that read Quiet, Genius at Work or I'd Rather Be Sailing and travel posters of the surf at Maui or Kauai.

There weren't any posters at Ann Hardy's cubicle. There were no photographs, not even a box of Kleenex. There was just Ann, lovely, sweet Ann, bent over her IBM terminal, her face reflected quietly in the tinted glass.

"Peek a boo," he whispered.

"Hello, Charlie," she said.

He had made it a point to stop at a few other stations on the way so that it was not a dead giveaway when he got to hers. The secret, he believed, was still preserved, and because he had vowed once upon a time never again to have anything to do with women at the office, he found himself wanting to ask everyone to stand up, please, out of those formica caves, he had an important announcement to make.

"Listen, all of you. Ann and I are screwing each other. We manage about every other Tuesday to get together at her place

13

after work to do it. I just thought you should know, that's all. To fill in your rosters."

"Is she any good?" John Sears, one of those with whom he had once tried to car pool, would ask.

"She's good, yes. A bit tentative and self-conscious, but when she gets close, she's pretty good then. Yes, good, I'd say. Any more questions?"

"Those boobs, are they real?" Marianne Kirsten would ask. She was flat chested.

"They're real, all right. You bet they're real. And how."

Her breasts, in fact, were what had made him break the vow in the first place. She had worked in the office three months, and he hadn't shown a shred of desire, even though he was delighted by how her stockings looked at the knee when she crossed her legs and how she smiled when she caught him staring.

He had been able to keep his vow, in other words--a vow established in good faith when the business with Arleen Boggiano, who worked in accounting, had terminated--until he rounded the corridor leading to the elevator one afternoon and stumbled directly into those two pillows of flesh. He experienced the oddest tingling, which travelled all the way from his neck to his heels and made his toes gather inside his wingtips.

It was an experience that enabled him to understand that he could endure any woman's presence, no matter how beautiful, so long as she did not touch him. Once that contact was made and he was forced to abandon the realm of vision, as in a motion picture theater, where illusion is enough, he felt a call so dark and primitive that it must be answered. It seemed the most natural thing to imagine lying next to a naked Ann Hardy, having a pleasant conversation and getting up and putting his clothes on. But if she should merely touch his shoulder with those long, succulent fingers....

14

That's why he never danced with anyone but Marian, anyone, that is, whose body could take his eyes to the movies.

She regarded him with something that was not quite enthusiasm. He felt cheated.

That feeling passed quickly when he saw the anguish in her face. He had not been with her long enough to withdraw any part of himself when these moments of self-analysis and pity came upon her. That a woman would feel such regret about fucking a married man in a town where half the men were queer and the other half had been divorced seemed a bit provincial, but Charlie was aware of the limits of his own permissiveness. There was in him someone who longed to stand at the corner of Market and Powell when the rain came down and offer an old woman an umbrella.

He bent into her cubicle and made his lips into a kiss.

"Lunch," he said. "One o'clock. OK?"

Her eyes got big. For a moment she seemed utterly oblivious and spread her legs against the swivel chair as though she were on the can. Her defenselessness made him want to take her in his arms and promise never to leave her.

"One o'clock," he said and stepped away.

Later he took a cab uptown and got out in front of Macy's. He bought Marian a silk scarf and had it sent to his office. Then he walked the extra block to O'Doul's. He had always liked the place because it reminded him of a San Francisco that didn't exist anymore.

"It was before my time, as they say."

A man and woman, who had arrived only the night before from Bakersfield, turned on the sidewalk and stared at him.

But there was an illusion of something in the old place, with the black and white photographs of dead ball players on the walls, the long, gleaming mahogany bar with the matching stools, the tables with cane back chairs and oilcloths, the bartenders with white towels around their waists, the deli where you stood in line for the corned beef and cabbage and particularly the lovely brown depth of the half light when you came in from the street. He could imagine another time, when women's dresses touched the floor and men's suits had too much material. She was waiting in a booth next to the wall.

"Hi," he said, bending over her. She moved her head just enough for him to miss her lips. He smelled the perfume under her ear and noticed that she had taken great care to have her makeup fresh and all the hair in place. She was wearing a dark suit that gave her blue eyes a kind of phosphorescence and her nails were perfect. All this contrasted with the vague sadness in her face, as though she had just come out of I. Magnin's and witnessed an accident in the street. He imagined that even Joan of Arc, before going to the stake, had asked for a mirror.

"What are you going to have?" he asked.

"A liverwurst," she replied. "And some cole slaw."

"Do you want a beer?"

"Would it be good with beer?"

"Why not?"

"Maybe some white wine, then."

"All right," he said. "Think nice thoughts while I'm gone, will you?"

He passed the waitress and ordered half a carafe of wine and a Corona for himself. Then he stood in line.

There were a dozen people in front of him, and he could see only her hands clasped nervously together on the table, like someone whose passport has been, for a moment, detained. He turned and looked through the open door.

Outside the air was as grey as the sidewalk. Pedestrians flicked by. When you saw them like that, just a glimpse, your eye was caught by only a detail, and you judged them by the fact that they wore sneakers without socks or carried a

16

shopping bag they had used over and over again or had hair that was bleached and ratted. The suit, a pinstripe, had no vest or was built up too much in the shoulders. The ankles were too fat or the face, glancing toward the sound of laughter from the bar, was too sallow or bland. The stride was all right or the color of the tie. The shoes were all right. So was the figure or the fit. The tilt of the head or the smile was all right. The world divided itself into two classes, affirmed out of a lifetime of experience, by a single glance. People were either assholes or they weren't. And most of them were assholes.

When it was his turn, he ordered corn beef and liverwurst from an ugly man with a tall, white hat flopped over one ear who growled, "What's yours?"

He had sympathy for such occupations. Car wash attendents, cashiers at mini-marts, change makers at Harrah's, carvers of roast beef at O'Doul's. Everything else worked because somewhere at the bottom they offered their lives between appetite and satisfaction. The orderly functioning of society was guaranteed by the swiftness of their hands or the sureness of their skill. In the most trivial service, they were toll gates you passed through without a second glance.

He carried the trays over to the booth and sat down. Her back was to the light that came in from the street, and when she leaned forward, her face seemed to lose some of its color.

"It's Tuesday," he said, trying to smile.

She looked up and nodded. She took a sip of wine and touched the liverwurst with the tip of her finger. "It's fresh," she said.

"If you knew Tuesday like I know Tuesday," he sang. It didn't work.

He wouldn't get angry. In a life that was so often banal and commonplace, he savored those moments when it became precious again. He could forget everything for a time

17

just sitting across from her. If only she would cooperate, all the routine could melt away. All the baggage he had to carry could be set down. It was all he asked of her, all he had asked of any of them, that they forget, just for a moment, the encumbrance of personality, the shackles of expectation and ambition. Simply the joy of driving that silver automobile through the streets, that was enough. Simply the pleasure of feeling her skin under his hands, her mouth against his face, that was enough too. Because a moment, a little goddamn moment, was all they allowed you.

Charlie believed that the one fear we all possess is the fear of being lost. He had learned the fear as a boy, when his mother had slept in the same room with his brother and him because his father was fucking another woman. The presence of his mother in the room at night gave the universe a twist. He lay awake at times listening to her breathing and feeling the odd, heavy sleep of her in the bed next to him. He thought of his father alone in the other room.

He had wet dreams in the blackness of his mother's sleep. He had learned to masturbate in the dark morning of her sleeping. He had lived some part of boyhood with the certainty that she would be asleep there beside him in the terror of his nightmares. And one night he had awakened and she was gone.

What he heard instead was the rhythm of his father's bed. What he listened to were the cries of his mother's pleasure.

"Oh, Daddy, Daddy, Daddy."

Had she forgotten who she was? Had she turned the universe upside down just to spill him out? Had they not all left each other to find separate ways, abandoned, like lifeboats from a sinking ship?

When she returned to the room carrying the smell of his father's cigarettes and a scent he had never before experienced, he lay awake as she went to sleep, and he felt the

18

loss.

He lifted his eyes from the corned beef, from which he had not yet taken a bite, and said, "I saw a woman commit suicide this morning."

"You what?" she said, looking straight at him. "Please don't be funny, Charlie."

"It's true. This morning. Coming to work. Her car stalled and she got out and jumped over the side."

"She jumped because her car was stalled."

"It was a Riviera. A green one."

"People don't kill themselves because their cars stall, Charlie."

"I'd like to believe that," he said, and put a forkful of cabbage into his mouth. She shook her head and turned to regard a little black man who, his hat between his teeth, was setting his tray down at the table next to them.

She was one of those women, he believed, who are never meant to live in the city. Such women arrive in a state of awe and wonder, find work and an apartment and spend the rest of the time trying to understand why they're so different. They drive the streets with the windows up and the doors locked and are angry at those who run intersections on the yellow light. They are bothered by strangeness, yet they walk the sidewalks looking straight ahead for fear they will see someone they know and be asked to have a drink. They enjoy shopping for bargains on Union Street or 24th, but you have the feeling they would be more comfortable at Mervyn's or Weinstock's. They have men and often marry, but they are never happy.

"We are going to be together this afternoon, aren't we?" Charlie asked. He wanted to use words that had air in them so that she could float comfortably.

But it was just such language that troubled her, for she seemed so much to drift lately. The whole city was a river

19

upon which she was drifting.

"All right," she said.

He didn't want to ask, "What's wrong?" and pin it all on something unanswerable. There was no finality and no solution to "What's wrong?" because there wasn't anything that could be right, not anything, leastways, that you could put your finger on. He would take "All right." He would enjoy her without having to know the answer to "What's wrong?"

Sometimes between those who are intimate a silence falls, like the silence after a closed door. He did not know what to say, and it troubled him that it might already have been said.

He stared at the room. The people were all naked, with dewlaps of fat and fallen breasts, bent toward each other, pushing food into their mouths and talking nonsense. He could see right through their gabardine suits and pleated skirts. Who the hell did they think they were? And why the goddamn hell did he spend hours and hours beside Marian on the couch watching the goddamn television when the whole goddamn earth was crumbling beneath the lawn outside and he was getting goddamn puffy under the eyes, thank you?

He looked at Ann, and there was a wildness in his look, for she drew back.

"Charlie, are you all right?"

"I'm fine," he said. "Just fine."

He put his napkin down and stood up. He walked around the booth to the stairs that led down a narrow corridor to the bathroom.

He pushed the door open and was greeted by an acrid smell that was wet and old. He went to a stall and unzipped his pants.

He always experienced the most generous sensations when relieving himself. Sitting on the toilet or standing

20

before a bowl, he felt the universe contract under the swell of his exertions, so that what remained was only this primitive creature, as ancient as time itself. Everything that lived excreted. In the rush of life there was this pause, where bowels and intestines ruled. The plans that were made, the nests that were under construction, the battles of fishes and lions and men, the lusts and loves and ambitions, all ceased before this descent into non-being. Nothing was as good as a good shit. It took all the pride away and joined the most humble native, squatting behind his hovel in the jungle, to someone as arrogant as Chris Carpenter himself, who owned the company and bought his suits at Merriwether's and his shirts at Bartholomew's. It was blissfully blind and divinely without reason. It was at the dawn and the sunset of creation. God himself must have gone to the head on the seventh day.

He watched the urine descend in a yellow arc. There was something in the light, in how, finally, only gulping drops came, one by one, to curve into obliteration that made him think about the woman going over the bridge.

Was she sorry she had laughed at him? Did his sticking his tongue out at her make her feel bad?

"Maybe she screamed. Maybe it was too much for her to scream." His voice echoed in the evil-smelling room. "Maybe she just fell, turning around and around, like. Maybe she was conscious." He shook his prick. "She would pull her arms and legs in if she were conscious, I bet. Maybe she'd try to fly, though, like a bat, maybe, or with the coat out, like a parachute. If she were conscious, that is, and changed her mind. Quick thinking, all right. But what a deal if you should change your mind going down."

He heard a shuffle in one of the stalls and the door opened. In that case, he finished thinking, better you should be a piece of shit.

He shook himself again as a rather thin-faced man with

close-cropped hair and slender wrists came up and stood beside him. The man was wearing a scarf tied round his neck and a grey woolen coat that came to his knees. The coat was buttoned all the way to his throat. He looked at the man, who stood smiling at him with perfect teeth and a kind of beatific expression of understanding.

"It's so terrible to be alone," the man said in a voice that made something crawl across Charlie's scalp.

"What was that?"

"Don't put it away," the man smiled. "Let me hold it in my mouth and I'll make you happy."

Charlie hesitated for an unbearble moment of stupefaction and fear, in which he and this person seemed to move toward each other in slow motion, for the man took the moment as acceptance and was already descending to one knee. Charlie stepped back, put his hand upon the man's head and shoved.

The man fell back, trying to catch his balance, and struck his chin against the urinal. He crumpled to the floor and blood came out of his mouth.

When Charlie got to the door, working so frantically at his zipper that he pulled it from the track, he turned around. The man was sitting on the cold tile floor of the bathroom, his legs straight out. Blood was dripping onto his scarf. He was crying.

CHAPTER THREE

The company had given top priority to the Eisner Corp merger, and while he glanced over the memos, his secretary fixed the zipper on his pants. In the meantime, Charlie wore a pair of bib overalls he had found in the custodian's closet.

He sat behind his desk with the door closed. There was a pale blue light in the room, and against the ceiling tiny glimmerings shone. The sun was on the bay behind him. If he looked out the window, he knew the afternoon would be lost.

He tried to concentrate on the memos. The Eisner deal was his baby, after all. He had done the paper work on the tender offer, which was reasonable at fifty-four dollars a share. Even Harry Eisner had thought so. Actually, the corporation could go for another ten dollars easy, but Eisner was a tired old fox who had been hunted one too many times, and all he wanted now was to play golf in the Bahamas, pump his new, young wife and give lectures at Columbia Business School. Even when some of the directors had rejected the friendly offer and threatened to take Eisner Corp private in a leveraged buyout, Eisner brought them around for sixty-two dollars a share and avoided the spear Carpenter was getting ready to throw at the common. Charlie had spent a lot of time over calamari at Scoma's playing every birdie the old man had ever made at Pebble or Spyglass to keep him more excited about fairways than phosphorous.

There is a time when a fellow should retire, that was the point. It wasn't an evil thing to play golf every day or sleep with the smell of perfume on your pillow rather than the vague scent of Clorox you found in those damned hotels.

"I'll miss the fight, though," Eisner had said. "But that's for you younger bucks now. Every old stag has to turn in his antlers someday."

Charlie didn't think the analogy apt but smiled. He found it peculiarly gratifying to hear the word "young" applied to him, in spite of the extra two letters. As for retirement, he felt only astonishment.

The idea of doing nothing bewildered him, and as he had watched David and Kelly gradually become larger, leaving clothing and objects behind to the miniaturization called childhood, the thought that he himself was no longer getting bigger but only older seemed cruel and unfair.

He had always worked, and though he had often been bored and even resentful, there was something compelling and necessary about what happened Monday through Friday. The determination of man was written in the stoplights he placed at his intersections. If there were no Monday through Friday, Saturday and Sunday would be meaningless.

Charlie looked at the old man, hunched down in his suit, his veined, paper-thin flesh colored like used marble, and was amazed. That life should have a destiny filled by this absurdity, that the old man should seek, in his last days, to fornicate like a bridegroom and worry over a shortened backswing, that such nonsense was, in fact, the sole purpose of his own 401K and the reason for these urges to visit the doctor, with the concern about smoking and cholesterol, fibre and weight, seemed as ludicrous as the notion, well, that he might live forever.

How many times had he and his brother Jack traveled the thousand miles to the Yellowstone and found the highway littered with those ugly, square boxes driven by balding men, their wives perched beside them like gnarled, grey parrots, a CB antenna waving above the roof, the saliva of dogs smeared upon the windows behind the dusty curtains and the motto stuck to the rear bumper: "We're spending the kids' inheritance"? It was the dream of every slob who earned less than $30,000 a year. Sell the house, buy a motorhome and see the world. Old man Eisner, fucking his golddigging wife on a waterbed in the Bahamas, and Clyde Lurch and the Missus, sucking beer and watching the portable Sony at an RV park somewhere near Couer d'Alene, it was all the same. And it frightened him.

He could not concentrate on the papers before him and he dare not turn around. There was a faint, antiseptic smell in the room, and he thought of Mrs. Bolkonski, who watered the plants each Tuesday. Mrs. Bolkonski's son had been killed in Vietnam, and she had gone to the memorial in Washington and run her fingers over his name and then bought a flower shop with the money the government had given her. But the smell was a little stronger than Mrs. Bolkonski, and he looked at the floor to see if it had been mopped. Then he realized it was the overalls.

He pushed the chair back from the desk. The overalls were soiled and there was a yellow stain on one knee. He felt quite silly sitting there in a pinstripe Nordstrom shirt and tie and two hundred and fifty dollar Mario Bruni shoes while over his shoulders he wore the straps of a worksuit some illiterate janitor had bought at Penny's.

He could feel the hair of his thighs against the heavy denim cloth. Another man had occupied the overalls, and as his flesh warmed the material, he was aware of a dull scent that made him uncomfortable. There was a cloying little shiver when he imagined where the other's legs had been. Into what evil had they carried him, or what pain? Were murder, rape and incest seeped within the threads and fibres? Were these crimes even now awakening along his calves and hips?

"Sonofabitch."

He stood up and searched through the pockets. There were a few matchbooks, which he read carefully. A toothpick. There was a small cloth that had been used to rub something so often that it was colored like the fingers of old women who play slot machines. In a chest pocket, where pencils and rulers should have been, he found the stub of a cigarette.

He removed it and as soon as he saw it, he realized that it was the remainder of a joint. He was putting it into his shirt pocket when the door opened.

"I had to see it," Frank said, grinning.

"So now you've seen it. So go away."

"The Attack of the Fly," Frank laughed. "What happened? Somebody catch you playing with yourself in the can?"

"That's closer than you think," Charlie said.

Frank came in and closed the door.

Charlie had never been able to make up his mind if he liked Frank Ruskin or not, but he supposed he didn't. Yet there was an immutable bond between them, whose origin lay in the fact that they had at one time screwed the same woman. At any staff meeting, any social function of the company, like a trip to the wine country or a cruise up the delta, they seemed to gravitate toward each other, and even when they stood apart, if they were in the same room together, he would look up and find Frank staring at him.

At first he had thought that it was because the woman, whom he had known as Julie Robardts, was actually Frank's wife. Not then, of course, because they had just gotten the

26

divorce before Frank came on board and Julie had taken her own name again, so how was he to know when he met her in the lobby of the building one day that she was the ex-wife of a company employee?

One evening Frank had come into the place over on Columbus where she liked to take him. He spotted them in a rear booth, walked over and sat down.

"Well, Julie," Frank said. "Old habits are hard to break."

"I still love the old place," she said.

"Sure. That Old World charm."

And then Frank had given him the look for the first time, which was something akin to the look one man gives another when they are bidding over a locked suitcase at an auction and each believes in a secret treasure.

"Charlie," Julie said, "Frank is my ex-husband."

He had felt very uncomfortable and thought about standing up and excusing himself, but Frank said, "Take it easy, old boy. That's water under the bridge. No problem. We're all adults here."

"Well," Charlie said, moving away from her a little, "I'm sorry, I guess." He felt as though he had stolen something at the drugstore and the clerk had followed him out into the street.

"We were separated eight months before I filed for the divorce," Julie said. "So you see, it's all ancient history, isn't it?"

Frank said. "And we're still friends, aren't we, Julie?"

"Of course."

"So why don't you let me buy you both dinner, and we'll have a nice talk?"

He stopped seeing Julie shortly after that, and then he came to realize that it had little to do with the fact of the marriage. It seemed to be more curiosity than anything else. They stood next to each other, as they were doing now, and longed to ask questions.

How was it? Did she do this or that? How did she respond? Did she come more than once? Let me tell you what happened, and then you tell me, and maybe we can learn something. Maybe if we pool our knowledge, maybe if we could get a half dozen other guys to screw her too, we could learn something really worthwhile about women.

At one time, when he was much younger, Charlie had thought that the avenues along which life is lived were rather simple and straightforward. You went to school, you learned the duly appointed skills, you went out and found a job and practiced the skills, you met a person whom you decided to marry and you had children. And then everything just got more.

Now he believed that life had a subterranean side about which he knew little at all, and there were passageways below that joined people in the strangest manner. Frank Ruskin and he would be brothers forever, as much as if they had been plucked from one ovum, and merely because they had gone into the same woman and found an absence of joy.

"Where are your pants?" Frank asked.

"Janet has them. She's working on the zipper. Damned thing just pulled off."

"What happened? Was it stuck?"

"Stuck, yes. Then I just jerked on it and the damned thing came off. I had to carry my coat in front of me."

Frank grinned. "What are you working on?"

"Going over my notes on the Eisner merger."

Frank walked over to the window and looked out. "You must be quite pleased with this one. You did quite a job. Eisner thinks you're his caddy."

"Isn't that swell."

"You really sold the deal."

He shrugged his shoulders and decided to give up and

walk over to the window.

It was a lovely afternoon. The sun was warm and golden on the bay. There was a special iridescence to the water. The color was so deep and perfectly blue that the sky looked pale and insignificant. A few sailboats were tacking about, making the turn toward Alcatraz.

"You're all set for the meeting, then," Frank said.

"As set as I'll ever be," Charlie replied.

"You'll get a promotion out of this, you know."

"I don't want a promotion."

Frank turned with an incredulous look, but he was no more surprised than Charlie.

"Did I hear you correctly? I'd give my left arm to be in your spot right now. You must be kidding."

"I don't think I'm kidding," Charlie said.

"You don't think you're kidding. C'mon. You shouldn't talk like that."

Charlie put the words into his mind and tried them out. Then he said, "I don't want a promotion." They sounded just fine, thank you.

Frank stepped back. "Are you feeling all right?"

"I'm feeling fine."

"You look a little puffier maybe. You putting on weight?"

"I'm not puffy, goddamn it. It's the overalls."

"Say, you are putting on weight. Sure you are. Now look at me." He slapped his waist. "I've lost ten pounds. Back into tennis after all these years. At our age a man has to start taking care of himself. You ever get tired?"

"I'm tired all the time, Frank."

"You're not getting enough exercise, that's what it is. Exercise and diet, they're the key. Regular exercise and weight control. How's the golf game?"

"My game's fine. Forget it, Frank. I'm all right."

"You're not all right if you're thinking of passing up a

29

chance to become a vice president."

"They wouldn't make me a vice president."

"Like hell they wouldn't. Now how much golf are you playing?'

"I'm playing enough."

"You should go out more. It's the Eisner deal. You're just strung out from putting it together. Listening to old man Eisner's stories would wear anybody down."

"I don't know why I said it. Forget it," Charlie declared.

"I'm not the one that needs to forget it."

"All right. I don't know why I said it. I've forgotten it." He smacked his forehead with an open palm. "There. It's gone."

"You must be crazy to pass up such a deal. Haven't you heard any of the rumors going around? You have a good chance for a vice-presidency."

"If you say so."

"You'd be crazy," Frank said, looking out the window. "I should have a chance like that. They could have both my arms for a chance like that."

"Then you couldn't play tennis, Frank."

They stared at the bay. He could hear Frank breathing.

"How long you been with the company now, Charlie?"

"Fifteen years."

"With me it's twelve. That's pretty close together."

"I guess so," Charlie said.

"We started out pretty much together, I mean."

Charlie didn't say anything.

"I'd come to work sometimes early and find that goddamned wagon of yours parked in the lot. I always thought you were the hardest working sonofabitch the company had. You still get here sometimes earlier than anyone else."

"It's the traffic on the bridge," Charlie said.

"The most hard working sonofabitch we had," Frank said,

taking a step closer to the window. "But you know what? I think you're lucky, that's all. That's the way it happens sometimes. Some guys are just lucky. I don't know what it is, but you're goddamn lucky."

He felt at that very moment, still after all those years, the desire to ask Frank about Julie. It seemed more important than anything else in the world to get whatever information they could out into the open.

"You know why I think you're lucky?" Frank said. "I think you're lucky because you don't really care, Charlie. There's something inside you I could never figure, but you don't take it seriously, not at bottom, I mean. You work hard, you work your fucking ass off. But right there at the core of the whole thing, you're not there. And I don't have that, Charlie. If that's what it takes, then I don't have it, because I care about this company more than anything else, more than my own personal life. Why do you think I've stayed single all these years after the divorce?"

Charlie looked at him but, Frank kept his eyes turned toward the bay.

"I'm not complaining, mind you. I've done all right and I'm not jealous, I don't think. I'm surprised, that's all. I simply don't understand. Because there must be a large part of us that's very much alike. You see that, don't you? We have to be the same largely in our appeal, I mean. You know what I'm talking about."

Frank wiped his lip and Charlie felt his heart quicken.

"It's just that there, right there, we're different. Why should some people get what they're not even looking for while others won't ever find what they've always wanted?"

Charlie said nothing. Instead he put his hands into the pockets of the coveralls and felt like a workman in another part of the world getting ready to clean up the mess made by tourists.

"That's the ugliest goddamn bridge," Frank said. "How do you stand looking at the goddamned thing every day?"

"It's not so bad," Charlie said. "In fact, I like that bridge."

"There, you see what I mean?" Frank tapped the window. "Say, you hear about that woman this morning?"

Charlie frowned. He decided he had nothing about that woman he wanted to talk to Frank about.

"What woman?"

"Right out there. Her car stalled and she just dove over the side."

"Is that a fact," Charlie said.

"I was listening to the stock market report before I came in. They had it on. She just dove over the side and broke her goddamn neck, I'll bet. They haven't found the body yet."

Charlie looked out at the blue water shining beneath the bridge. "I hadn't heard," he said.

"Her car stalls and she kills herself."

Charlie was staring at the point where the Coast Guard boat had circled.

"You ought to take up running maybe. Carpenter himself is taking up running. It's great exercise. That's what you need. That's what we all need. Anyone would give his eye teeth to be a vice-president. That's why we're here, isn't it? Just get rid of a little fat, that's all."

Charlie was staring at the water. It was not possible, of course. The current would have carried the body far away. But right there, shining in the afternoon sun, seemed to be a patch of something red.

* * *

Ann Hardy had a nice one-bedroom apartment on Diamond Heights. The view was not toward the City but toward the west and a rugged little canyon down which an occasional hawk flew. Often it would be warm in the financial district, but by the time he got up to her place, there would be the fog and a twenty-degree drop in temperature. He enjoyed looking out the windows at the canyon. He could see the cross in the pines on Mt. Davidson above all those crackerbox houses and the red-legged broadcasting tower on Twin Peaks. To the far left he could glimpse, when the weather was clear, a blue corner of the Pacific and a ship moving out to sea.

When Ann opened the door that afternoon, she had already changed into the faded yellow dress that depressed him so much. She had kept it from an earlier life and trotted it out whenever she felt sulky or ashamed. When he stooped to kiss her and she held her lips together, he knew he had his work cut out for him.

"You're feeling all right, aren't you?" he said.

That was enough to let her know he was concerned for her but not enough to let her off the hook.

"I'm a little tired," she said.

"You need to lie down and relax." He kept his arm about her, down along her side, his hand on her hip. He could feel her underpants beneath the thin dress.

"I'm not sure what I need."

He squeezed her and smiled. He would not bite on anything. He was as resolved as an executioner. How much of life depended upon resolution, upon not surrendering to those hints for mercy that sprang up everywhere. Yet, as he led her to the bedroom, he felt a distance, as though he were watching it on film.

"We're always in a hurry," she said. "Why do we have to always be in a hurry?"

He wanted to glance at his watch but decided against it. He could tell from the position of the sun that it was somewhere around four-thirty. He had to be on the bridge by six at the latest.

"I don't see it as hurry," he said. "You know I wouldn't

want to hurry."

"Why wouldn't you want to?"

"Because I love making love with you. I wish it could last all night."

"You would like to make love to me all night, Charlie?"

"At least."

"What's our record?"

"What do you mean?"

"For making love."

"Well, let's see. There was that meeting at the Meridian a month or so back. We had to stay late. That was a few hours, wasn't it?"

"Yes. You loved me for a few hours. I remember."

They were up against the bed and he had his arms around her.

"How's your family?" she asked.

"Oh, they're fine," he said. "Thank you."

"And your wife, how is she?"

"I included her in the 'they're fine.' "

"Will she be waiting dinner for you to get home?"

"I don't know. It depends. Sometimes she waits and sometimes she doesn't."

"Do you like sitting down and having dinner with them?"

"It's all right sometimes. Sometimes it isn't."

"Charlie, why are we together?"

He felt his heart beating. She wanted him to step back, and then all the words would start.

He tried to kiss her. She moved her head, but he took her chin in his hand and held her still. He pressed his lips to hers and she made a little sound like something trapped under a basket. He began to pull the dress up over her hips, and she pushed at his hand. The dress tore.

The sound of the fabric made him see just why he longed for these little forays into the bodies of beautiful women.

34

There was something right about walking into a strange bedroom, dropping your pants, staying around for an hour or two and then leaving. A vision crossed his mind. He saw himself high up in the Sierra. It was early spring and the snow was melting and he was coming down out of the dark trees into a clearing where all the does were. He was a stag who had wandered alone through the silence of winter and now he was coming down to them and they were all waiting in no particular order, and he would have them that way and, finally, he would return to the wilderness.

The image thrilled him. Between his legs was the very power of nature, the instrument that made life run, and it was as unmarried and impersonal as the sun, drifting into the cold Pacific.

At the sound she took her hand from his and allowed him to pull the garment over her head. He loved undressing her. Sometimes, when they walked into the apartment together and she had everything on from work, he would take his time removing it all. The flesh appeared, bit by bit, like some precious gift that had been expensively wrapped, and when she stood naked before him, he had been given something he had never dreamed of possessing.

He turned her around and unhooked the bra. Her back had a beautiful, long arch. Then he slid her silk panties down and ran his hands over her hips, along her legs to her ankles. Kneeling, he turned her around and kissed her stomach. He stood up and unzipped his pants.

When it was finished, when she had come and he had come and they lay there on her salmon colored sheets, she turned to him and said, "I don't think we should do this anymore, Charlie."

He looked at her. Always after an orgasm his mind went cold, and for a time it was as though he would never need a woman again.

35

"I mean I want it and enjoy it and when I'm into it there's nothing I want more. But, Charlie, I just don't want this anymore. Do you understand?"

The pale light, moving in through the curtained windows, made little hollows beneath her breasts. Her body was very lovely.

"You're saying goodbye again."

"No, I'm not saying goodbye again. I'm saying goodbye. We're not going anywhere, Charlie."

"Going anywhere. Why do we have to go anywhere? Why can't we be where we are?"

"Just enjoy what we have, just enjoy it for the moment, and you go on home to the wife and kids while I douche, eat a TV dinner and catch the ten o'clock news before bed. Is that it?"

The coldness, it seemed, had run all the way from his brain to his feet.

"What are you so worked up about?" he said. "You act as if something has surprised you. You knew what to expect when we started this."

"Why did we start, Charlie?"

"Oh," he said. "You did expect something else."

She didn't say anything, but pulled the sheet up to her chin.

"I didn't understand," she said, "that you just did this. I thought there was something about me, just me, since you wanted so much to have me. But there wasn't. We just have our routine. And that's what it is. Our routine. Every other Tuesday or so."

"Don't you have a career?"

She stared at him.

"There was something about you," he said, but stopped.

He felt the words beginning to arrange themselves. He could lay them all out for her, build a nice structure of confidence and desire. Maybe he could even convince her for next week. But he was so cold he would never need to come again, not ever. If he were alone in the world with millions of women and they were all waiting for him in the clearing, he would never need to leave the mountains again.

She looked at him. "You're so unhappy, Charlie, and now you've made me unhappy too. Why are you so unhappy?"

The word sounded strange to him.

"You don't love me, Charlie. You fuck me." She turned on one elbow to face him. "I like fucking you. When we're into it, I truly enjoy it. When we first started, I loved just being with you, and when we were together, all I wanted to do was be in bed with you, because it was just a part of everything else. But after awhile I realized what was happening and I separated out what we do in bed from everything else and I lived for that. But it didn't work because I didn't feel worthy, if you can understand that. After awhile fucking you became like fucking myself, and I could do that alone."

"Everybody fucks everybody."

She got up and went to the closet. She put on a purple satin robe he had not seen before. Then she switched on the lamp. He wiped himself with the sheet and stood up. He could not remember anything about any joy they might have experienced. She seemed rather bizarre and alien, standing against the closet door in her new shining robe and painted toe nails. The worst thing that ever happened to love, he decided, was speech. They should have banned talking between men and women a long time ago.

"I will not believe that," she said.

"You mean you can't believe it."

"You must think I'm just a country girl lost in the big city."

"I come from a little valley town too."

"I'd leave and go back in a minute if I thought what you

said is true."

"Why didn't you just tell me you were seeing other men?"

She was startled and he began to draw on his pants.

"Just one," she said. "How did you know?"

"Call it men's intuition."

"I thought at first," she said, "that I shouldn't. I sat here after you left and thought I shouldn't. But I haven't gone to bed with him. I couldn't."

"But now it's down to that. So to speak."

"I guess it is."

"Watch out," he said.

"What do you mean?"

"The city," he said, buttoning his cuffs.

She stared at him. "You truly need something, Charlie. You're a lonely man."

"I resent being singled out," he said. He drew on his socks and laced his shoes. He went over to the mirror above the dresser and knotted the tie beneath his collar. He could see her reflection in the glass. With her arms crossed and her feet naked, she looked like something that had been pulled out of the water at Seal Rock.

"Do you love anything, Charlie?" she asked.

"That question doesn't mean anything," he replied.

She stared at him. "I don't believe what you just said."

"Why? Does it take something away from what we've shared?"

"Don't you at least have children? Don't you have a mother?"

She discreetly had left out his wife. "All of those," he said.

"Don't you love them?" She seemed a little frantic.

"I haven't thought about it," he said. "Not lately anyway. I couldn't give you an answer." He studied himself in the mirror. He brushed his hair with his fingers.

38

She stepped toward him. Her hands were making little waving motions. "But didn't you love your wife when you married her?"

She sounded like Marian, desperate about his health.

He tried to remember when he had proposed to Marian. It was a long time ago. He was young. It was after a party and they had taken off their clothes in the back seat of the Plymouth parked behind the piracantha at the country club. He remembered that it was summer because they weren't cold and the seat had felt tacky under his legs and there was no moon.

It had been very dark in the back seat against the piracantha, but he could see her teeth and the whites of her eyes. Then there was something funny about the sound their bodies made rubbing against the seat, and they were still laughing and she couldn't come because the more they moved, the more sound they made, until he went ahead anyway, and later when he took her home, she began to cry, and so he asked her to marry him.

"No," he replied.

She turned away from him and he went into the living room to get his coat.

"Did you want to have lunch tomorrow?" he asked. He waited a moment and then opened the door.

Anyway, it was only a matinee. All he had to do was go outside and let his eyes get used to the light.

CHAPTER FOUR

There was a story in the paper the following morning and a picture of the Coast Guard cutter circling beneath the bridge. There was also a photograph of the woman. Next to the photograph was an article about the Ku Klux Klan.

"I'll be damned," he said.

"What's wrong, Daddy?"

He looked at the face of his daughter. It was the face that an angel might have, if there were such things. White and so clean and unblemished that it seemed almost two dimensional, the face had the frightening quality that beauty takes on when thought appears. From time to time her eyes would glaze, right there above her Quaker Oats, and a tiny furrow, like a crack, would open between her brows. It was a rift through his own heart. Something was happening down inside, in that invisible realm where he could not reach, and it made him feel helpless and old. Of all of them, Kelly was the one he truly had felt something for. Her vulnerability, her doll-like brittleness, which a year or two ago . . . what was it . . . ? she had laid aside in a corner of her closet with the rest of childhood, had given way to an opaque film that she

41

colored at the cheeks with a bit of rouge, and it seemed inevitable that one day she would become as hard-minded as her mother.

"Nothing, Kitten," he said. "Just something here in the paper."

He glanced at David, whose mottled face had the appearance of chewed pencil erasers, and tried to smile. David shifted his eyes.

He did not like his son. The antipathy had started someplace back in the sixth or seventh grade when he realized that he had spoiled him and then began holding it against him.

He did not believe in indulgence. He had said so often enough anyway, quoting chapter and verse from the scripture of his own boyhood. His mother had had to steal coins from his father's pocket while he shaved in the kitchen. He himself had had to work in an ink factory every afternoon to help pay his way through Berkeley. The hard lessons of life had been translated into an adulthood that found a much higher than average degree of success, and when David came into the world, he saw the infant, lying helpless in its own excrement, as an opportunity for moral revenge.

This son would know the difference between work and slavery. This son would discover that respect was a virtue. This son would not be deprived of the amenities of youth but would have them as the reward for responsibility and a job well done.

But what he did was give David all the pleasures and none of the obligations. Chores were not meted out consistently, so chores were accomplished haphazardly. An orderly room was demanded but not frequently enough inspected. Sloppiness was cleaned up by someone else. Failures were confused with successes. So that by the time he had reached middle school the boy had substituted television for reading and acoustics for writing, and from then on it was all downhill. Out of the resentment for his childhood and the subsequent guilt concerning his son, Charlie had created his own self-centered, shallow-witted, lackluster father, all over again.

He recognized the woman in the photograph. He had seen her sometimes buying meat at the Petrini's in Pleasant Hill. She had left a note on the seat of the Riviera, just one sentence: "I can't run anymore."

"How's the English going?" he asked.

His son turned a weak grin to him that he had been practicing for years.

"OK," David said.

"Daddy, I got an A on my history essay about saline injection and vacuum aspiration," Kelly said. Her face wore that bright look of insolent pride he had come to dread.

"Vacuum . . . ?"

"Abortion," Marian mouthed over her section of the paper.

He sighed. It was the same sigh he used when the lawnmower wouldn't start or the shower drain got clogged. "That's fine ," he said. "You know, Kel, aren't there some other things you could write about?"

"What do you mean, Daddy?"

"You know, other issues. Things beside this abortion business. Don't you think you're becoming a bit one-sided?"

"About abortion?"

"No, no. I mean that it's just that you seem only to be concerned about that one issue most of the time. Know what I mean?"

He was stepping on eggshells. David smiled maliciously at his sister, and her face puffed up even more.

Marian shook her head declaratively and, since the children were momentarily distracted, he said, "Fuck you," over the front page.

43

"Abortion is very, very important," Kelly said. "It's very, very terrible."

"That may be," he said, "but, Kelly, you're fourteen."

"What do you mean, Daddy?"

"Nothing. I mean you're fourteen, that's all."

"There's a girl in my home room who's thirteen, and her parents just made her have an abortion."

"Thirteen?" he said.

"Her name is Holly Westphal and she was pregnant and she had an abortion. And I think that's terrible."

"Jesus Christ, thirteen."

"They dump babies into buckets. They cut them up. Sometimes their heads get squeezed off. Sometimes. . ."

"Kelly, that's enough," her mother said.

". . .they're stuck into jars."

Charlie's heart was pounding. Had reality come so soon for this lovely child? Had the awful truth of things become so clear that there was no room left for fantasy or dream, only the brute certitude of fetuses stuffed into garbage cans?

"I have to go to school now," Kelly said.

He looked at his watch. "You're a little early, aren't you?"

"It's her stupid prayer meeting," David said. "They all hold hands in a circle for fifteen minutes every morning before class and pray."

"It's not stupid," Kelly declared, standing. "It's important. It's very important. Somebody has to do something. You ought to pray," she insisted, "with some of the things you do."

"What's that supposed to mean, Saint Kelly?" David glared.

"And don't call me that." Her face was red and her lower lip trembled.

"Stop it, David," his mother said.

"It's life," she cried bitterly. "It's the most precious thing and you just laugh at it. You don't care. Why should

44

somebody be allowed to take life away?"

"We care, Kitten," Charlie said. "Sit down now. Wait a minute. We care."

"Don't have a cow," David said.

"Shut up," said Charlie. He held his daughter's arm. "Sit down, Kel. Have another piece of toast or something. Of course we care."

He would not release her, and for a moment the entire family seemed frozen about the kitchen table. Time stopped and he had the weird notion that he could run it backward, and each of them, all of them together, might return to a photograph he remembered.

Something had gone wrong. Something terrible. But he couldn't put his finger on it. He couldn't say just what it was. It had come upon them slowly, as the seasons come, and here it was winter and they were wearing the wrong clothes.

"They'll be waiting for me, Daddy," Kelly said.

He let go of her arm.

"All right," he said. "You run along and pray, then. Pray for the unborn. That's what you're doing, isn't it?"

"Yes, Daddy."

"You stand together near the flag pole?"

She nodded.

"Is the flag up on the pole?"

"I think so, Daddy. I never really noticed."

"Well, pray for them, then. Pray for every goddamn one of them, you hear?"

She backed away.

"Pray for them to be born with no interference. That's fine," he said. "No whatchamacallit vacuum and no injections. Just right out there because it's god's will, that's what it is. Isn't it?"

"Charlie," Marian declared.

"Let them come on out, praise the lord. Come out, come

out, wherever you are."

"Charles!"

"And while you're at it, say a little something for the already born, won't you? A little something for your poor father here, that's all." He stood up, waving the newspaper.

Kelly ran into the dining room. He rushed after her and threw his arms around her.

"Daddy, what's wrong?" she begged, almost in tears.

"I don't know," he said, holding her. "I'm sorry. Listen, I'm sorry. I just want you to pray for me a little. Will you do that?"

"Daddy, you're scaring me. Please. Let me go."

Then she was out the front door and down the steps. He stood on the threshhold a moment, watching her disappear into the fog. He closed the door and returned to the kitchen.

"Christ Almighty, what was that all about?" Marian said. "You frightened her half to death."

He shrugged and looked at his son.

"Maybe you should see a psychiatrist today and not an M.D., for chrissake."

"What do you mean, OK?" Charlie said.

"What?" David replied.

"You said English was 'OK.' What do you mean, OK?"

Suddenly he was filled with a hatred that was as blind as his fear. He glared at David and recalled that Marian had not wanted to be pregnant. It had been a weekend at Carmel and she had not wanted a baby, and it had only been later, when Kelly arrived, that she grew reconciled to being a mother. He had not been concerned about such things, of course. He had just fucked her all weekend, and there she was missing her period with that odd, pointed look in her eyes.

"It's all right," David said. "I'm doing all right. Shit, Dad."

"All right, is it? It's always all right, isn't it? And then it's

46

shit, all right."

His rage made him helpless. When the boy was younger, there had been the sense that something could be improved. But now he was confronted by a will that was like a blunt instrument. He could not reason with David and could do nothing to him. David was just his son and he was just David's father.

"I'm going to work," he said, and walked out of the house.

* * *

He stood at the window looking at the bay. He was still holding the front page of the paper.

There was a peculiar translucence to the air, a combination of fog and sunlight and the emission of engines. Berkeley was wrapped by a buttery grey.

Her name was Ruth Danilow and there was a picture of her, a kind of owlish face with square, oversize glasses, loose, curling hair and a puckish grin.

"What in the hell is she grinning for?" Charlie said aloud.

She was a social worker and political activist and married to some crazy who had done demonstrations in the sixties and she had once placed second in the Boston Marathon and there were no survivors, only her husband, Abraham, who declined any comment about the fact that yesterday morning, in rush hour traffic, his wife Ruth had stopped her car on the Oakland-San Francisco Bridge and killed herself by doing a bellyflop into the Pacific Ocean. No funeral service was pending because they hadn't found the body, and then there was a list of activities: equal opportunity, fair housing, gay rights, NOW and an environmental group opposed to industrial pollution by Bay Area companies. Some of the companies were mentioned. One of them was Eisner Corp.

Charlie read the article five more times sitting in his chair with his back to the window. He remembered her from the aisles at Petrini's, a slender, small-breasted thing with a firm

47

ass. She hung about the coffee beans and herbal tea, one of those bright little women you'd never bother saying hello to.

The mystery of death had never puzzled Charlie, and suicide was something young Japanese pilots did in black and white movies made in the '40s. Uncle Nathaniel had shot himself twelve years ago, but he had only seen Uncle Nathaniel once, when he was five and his father had allowed his uncle to visit the house for a few hours before he left for Australia, so the news of his death was less strange than the odd-looking stamp that had been glued to the envelope.

"She must have lived pretty close," Charlie said, "for me to have seen her all those times. She could have lived a few minutes away. Maybe closer." He looked at the owlish face and the loose, curling hair. "Jesus Christ," he said. "Jesus H. Christ."

Charlie had to go to the meeting, but the incident with his family had left him vulnerable and depressed. He wondered if all that with Ann yesterday had been a game, and against his better judgment, walked past her desk. But she was gone. He sighed and took the elevator up to Carpenter's office.

He hated meetings. They were like ritual displays of animals in heat. The people bored him, and because he pretended to be interested, he went away from them with a headache and a vague sense of disgust which, at lunch, over a few gin and tonics, turned into humorless disbelief.

Carpenter's office took up three windows on the east side, and he enjoyed the view each time he came into it. Several stories higher added a dimension to the bridge that was lost from his window below. Maybe it was the extra glass, but the cables were more symmetrical and the ships passing beneath were less betrayed by the open sea.

"Well, now we're all here," Carpenter said as he entered.

The room had an antiseptic, bright quality, like a hospital corridor, and Carpenter's desk, which had a white formica top with a long, rectangular extension, filled much of it. Ten matching leather chairs were stationed about the table, and seated in one of them was old man Eisner, his back to the windows. The old man motioned to him and Charlie went over and sat down.

There were a couple of Eisner men he didn't recognize, but Bill Higgins was there from Research and Tom Couples and Fred Southworth from Sales. Larry Herzog from Personnel and Bill Spears and Ed McKnight from Advertising. He was surprised to see Kurt Arakawa from Legal. That meant something big was in the wind, and he found himself mildly curious.

"Gentlemen," Carpenter said, "this meeting will be brief. It's more a celebration and a recognition than anything else. A celebration first of our company's merger with Eisner Corp, a firm whose excellence in the field of bio-technology has long been recognized and whose president and owner, Harry Eisner, is here with us this morning."

There was a smattering of applause and Eisner smiled and showed Charlie his hands, which were gripping a putter. "Pebble," the old man whispered. "This afternoon."

"And a recognition," Carpenter went on, "because we're going to need a team to run the Eisner division of the company now, and, with the addition of one or two other men who couldn't be here because of pressing company obligations, you gentlemen will make up that team."

Carpenter paused to allow the importance of his words to sink in. With the exception of Eisner, everyone looked at the others. The old man waggled the putter. "Can you get away, Charlie?" he whispered.

"And one of you will have the opportunity to head the Eisner division of this company."

In the stunned silence Charlie could hear the old man breathing. Because of his connection to Eisner, the eyes of the others flicked to him.

"Quite frankly, anyone of you could run this company, and so the man who does must have more than just managerial skills. He must bring something more to running than business know-'how. In the next few weeks, I want each of you to think of just how you would handle the job and in what manner you would run the firm. Then I will talk to you individually and a decision will be reached. This may seem like an unorthodox procedure, but, gentlemen, we live in unorthodox times. Innovation equals survival. I wish you all luck. And now I'd like to ask Mr. Eisner if there is anything he wants to add. Harry?"

The old man stood and brandished the putter above the table.

"I always liked a good fight, boys," Eisner said. "Life ain't anything without a good fight. That's why we're in business, ain't that so? A good fight, that's our life's blood. It's what makes us go. Competition. Beating out the other sonofabitch before he beats you."

Eisner swung the putter and Charlie was amused at the affectation. "It puts the other fellow off his guard," the old man had told him one afternoon on the golf course, "so he'll come at you and you can see what he's made of, and then you can nail the sonofabitch."

The old man's eyes swept the room. "Of course, boys, I come from the Old School, but Carpenter is right. These are unorthodox times. There ain't an enterprise in this country today that don't have some damned do-gooders after it. Why, a man can't even pee on the ground without some mop-haired, braless, narrowchested bitch willing to lie down in the road to keep him from doing it."

The Carpenter people were not used to Harry Eisner, and Charlie watched the old man's eyes squint for signs of shock or weakness. The Eisner men were smiling.

"Why, you'd think it was 1967 all over again. Free enterprise is anti-American or some damned thing. We have to worry about some goddamn bird or some fucking, needle-nose fish whose name you can't even pronounce more than giving folks jobs and pushing this country forward. Environmentalists. Activists. Humanitarians. Civil libertarians. I'd like to give them their liberties right up here." He thrust the putter over the table. "They got us painted as bad guys, boys. Ain't that a rag? Us, who have a payroll of a million smackers a month." The old man snorted. "What this company needs now is a public image. It's public relations these days, boys. Everything is public relations. We need someone who can get these goddamned do-gooders off our backs and polish up our image."

There was a chuckle at the old man's elbow, and one of the Eisner men, a short, dumpy fellow wearing a seven hundred dollar suit, said, "Well, Mr. Eisner, if we could get them to all jump off the bridge, our problems would be solved."

The old man broke into uproarious laughter. The putter swung in a dangerous arc. The others about the table exchanged confused glances. Charlie sat forward and stared at the old man.

"I've said my say, boys. It's your fight now. This firehorse is out to pasture. The world just ain't the same. I don't like the rules nowadays. It takes a different breed of men. Actuality Training and Consciousness Raising. Buzzwords and bullshit. I'll be watching to see how you're doing, though, and dropping by from time to time. But I ain't worried. You'll do the job."

Eisner sat down and Carpenter had a half dozen bottles of iced champagne brought in. As the glasses were being filled, Charlie tapped the old man on the shoulder.

"Mr. Eisner," he said. "That remark about jumping off the

bridge, was that in reference to the Danilow woman who committed suicide yesterday?"

The old man's eyes lost their contrived narrowness. Instead they opened to reveal hard grey irises. "So what?" he said.

* * *

When he got back to the office, the phone was ringing.

"Guess what we just got in the mail," Marian said.

Charlie was a bit dazed. He said, "What did you say?"

"In the mail. It was just delivered. Another present from your son. A deficiency report."

"What's a deficiency report?"

"We called them cinch notices."

Charlie sighed.

"David is now failing English," Marian said.

Charlie did not say anything. He was thinking about fishing in Montana with his brother. There was a fine stretch of water on the Boulder River that an old guy named Virgil Bronson owned who had lived there since childhood. Virgil was eighty now and his land went two and a half miles along the river where big browns came out at dusk. Charlie held the receiver in his hand, and he could see the rings the big fish left in the flat water rising to dun colored insects that came down when the air was cool. Then, with the sun completely gone and only that whiteness against the darkening sky, he would hold a tiny flashlight between his teeth to tie on a fresh artificial fly because something unspeakable had snapped his line with one twist of its fearsome head. And by the time they hiked back to the pickup, the stars would be shining and they had to be careful driving the gravel road back to town because the deer were out and might jump against the cab of the truck.

"I've made an appointment with David's counselor today after school," Marian said.

"All right," he said.

"You'll have to keep it, Charlie. With a Mrs. Chalmers. It's at three o'clock. I can't make it."

"For chrissake, I don't want to see any goddamn counselor. Three o'clock. I'll have to leave work early. Why the hell can't you do it?"

"Charlie, you have a doctor's appointment at four. You have to be home early anyway."

"Well, why can't you see this counselor?"

"I told you. I can't make it. I've got to go to the hospital to see Mother."

"Another turn for the worse, I suppose."

"Well, that's a helluva concern on your part."

"I don't want to be lectured by some goddamn female counselor."

"You want to help your son, don't you?"

"Let's not get into it."

"It's settled then?"

He didn't say anything.

"The counseling office at the high school. Three o'clock. Mrs. Chalmers."

He imagined a twenty-inch rainbow leaping up from the dark surface of the stream, shaking the hook in its jaw, but something in the fading light that touched the pink silvery body made him think of a woman in a red suit going over a bridge.

"What are you home for now anyway?" he wanted to ask, but she had already hung up.

Charlie went to the window. In the late afternoon, a yellow luminescence lay upon the cold blue water. It was as though the bay had been covered by Saran. He looked down at the street seventeen stories below. Someone was jogging along the sidewalk against the traffic. He could see the top of his head and the flap flapping of his feet striking the

53

pavement.

"Maybe I could make it up to Ann," he said into the room, because now lunch lay ahead, like a foreign city in which he had no guide.

* * *

It was one of those schools named for a president. They were all named for presidents or towns or local dead who had made some contribution to community life. Golf courses were named the same way.

He parked the BMW in a visitor's stall, being careful to position it so that some bastard couldn't throw open a door and dimple his fender.

At three o'clock classes would be out for the day, and he was glad for that. There was something unnerving about hordes of adolescents milling around together. They reminded him of termites or soldier ants, gleeful and destructive at the same time.

The buildings of the school were familiar enough, long, rectangular shapes with rows of windows. Grass. A great deal of grass. Fruitless mulberry trees. Pines planted in tripods. A silvery pole two stories high flew the flags of California and the United States.

"So that's where Kelly prays."

He went across the parking lot and onto a concrete walk. Suddenly a group of students burst out of a door to a large brick building on his right, and he heard the sound of horns and woodwinds. The music had a sweet, almost played quality, but he was struck by the melody. It was Glenn Miller's *In The Mood.*

He went over to the building and looked through a window. It was a band or orchestra room of some sort. Folding chairs were spread in concentric circles, and a dozen or so kids were sitting there playing of all things Glenn Miller. He pressed his nose to the glass. The room was soundproof and he could just catch the rise and fall of the melody, and then something touched his heart and his eyes filled.

What was a bunch of kids these days doing playing Glenn Miller, who was even before his time, but whose music he had always loved? There was something he had just missed, and these kids had no idea of it at all, yet here they were playing *In The Mood* and not bad at that.

"Ta ta dah ta ta..."

Something like generosity filled Charlie's soul. A plague had swept the land, carrying everything before it, and the struggle to survive was taking on proportions beyond anyone's expectations.

"Ta dah ta dah ta dah dah dah."

Charlie tapped his finger against the window pane.

"And here these goddamn kids are playing Glenn Miller, like there's a secret we're all trying to remember."

Charlie was smiling more than he had smiled in a long time.

"I beg your pardon," a voice said at his elbow, "but may I help you?"

He turned to find a sallow-faced man in a polyester shirt and paisley tie. The man was wearing saddle oxfords and doubleknit slacks.

"Did you need some assistance?" the man asked.

Charlie stepped away from the building, and the music was lost in the brick walls.

"I have an appointment," Charlie said. "In the counseling office."

"Do you know where that is?" the man said.

"Well, no. I was here a year ago for freshmen orientation. My daughter. But, no, I don't know where the counseling office is."

The man turned sideways and pointed. "Straight ahead

there is the principal's office. Go around to the right of that. You'll see an air conditioning blockhouse. Pass to the left of that and keep straight ahead. You'll run right into the counseling office. There's a sign over the door."

"And the sign says?" Charlie asked.

The man looked at him. "Counseling," he said.

"I just wanted to be sure," Charlie said. "The sign above the principal's office there says 'administrative services.' " He walked away. When he rounded the corner of the building, he said, "Pompous sonofabitch."

Two girls turned to stare at him.

The counseling office door was made of glass with a metal bar for a handle. The glass panels next to it ran floor to ceiling and were filled with chicken wire. There were posters scotchtaped to the panels advertising dances, university applications and club meetings. He pushed the handle and went in. The clock upon the far wall said 3:10.

There were desks to left and right and a row of chairs under the glass panels. The smell of cheap perfume filled the air. Behind the desk on the left sat a skinny brunette with a long nose. At the desk on the right was a chubby faced blonde in a tight sweater. He took a guess.

"Pardon me," he said to the desk on the left, "but I have an appointment for three o'clock with a Mrs. Chalmers."

"Over there," the skinny woman said. "Miss Reilly will help you for juniors and seniors. I have the freshmen and sophomore counselors."

He took three steps and repeated his sentence. "One moment," the chubby faced woman said. She picked up the phone and spoke into it so that he could not hear. A young girl came out of a hallway and smiled at him. Her mini-skirt was so tight that Charlie swallowed and straightened his tie. He smiled back. The girl walked past him and out the door, and he had to fight the impulse to turn around and look at her calves.

A tall black woman with large breasts came out of the hallway. She saw him and manufactured a smile. "Mr. Bredesen?" she said. "I'm Vivian Chalmers, David's counselor. Why don't we go on back to my office?"

"All right," he said.

She was not wearing a wedding ring. It was the first thing he noticed about every woman he met.

He was not startled that she was black, and yet he was surprised. There were a few blacks in Walnut Creek, but not so you could notice, and it was his impression that they were doctors or lawyers or businessmen. There were virtually no Hispanics and he never saw any of those short, flat nosed types from Laos or Vietnam or Cambodia. It was odd, but as he sat in the chair she pointed to and watched her open a manila folder, he saw himself driving around the streets or walking through Nordstrom and everybody was white. It didn't seem to be any striking thing, but they were white all right, every damned one of them. Even the sales clerks and garbagemen and purveyors of hamburgers were white. It was a damned white community, and he stared at the black woman seated an arm's length away from him and thought, my son, the fuck-up, has a black counselor. It seemed somehow just right, and he smiled.

At that moment she raised her head and was confronted by the face of a man she had never seen before whose mouth was open and whose expression was one of guileless delight. She was totally unprepared for this and smiled in return.

Jesus Christ, he thought. She's beautiful.

"It seems David's having problems with his English," she said.

He lowered his eyes and then raised them. She was trying to make her voice pleasant, but he felt as though everything she said was aimed directly at him. His dislike for his son rose another notch.

But while his eyes were down, he had noticed that her shoes were made of some exotic skin, lizard, or maybe alligator.

"He's been telling me things were going better. Since his teacher called us, I mean."

"He's failing, Mr. Bredesen. If he fails, he won't graduate."

"What do you mean, just because of one lousy class?"

"The district requires the successful completion of four years of English. Mr. Walker is the one you should be talking to, but your wife was so insistent this morning, and Mr. Walker did have an important meeting."

"Sure, sure," he said. His eyes flicked about the room. It was a tidy place. The file cabinets, a dull beige, matched the desk. There was a porcelain vase with fresh carnations and a small jar of the ubiquitous jelly beans. A two-tiered book case contained copies of the state education code and a group of blue binders, neatly together with white labels. The window above the desk had chintz curtains. There was a brass trophy on the desk in the form of a woman running.

"My dear wife doesn't like loose ends."

She turned her head a little and regarded him.

"You know," he said. "Even keel. Don't rock the boat. Like that."

"I see," she said.

"No surprises, in other words." He looked at her. "Listen, what's your first name?"

"It's Vivian," she said.

"Listen, Vivian, I'm Charlie," he said, "and I want to believe my son when he tells me he's doing better in school. You understand? Maybe I don't believe him. But I just go along with it. We both go along. That way we can live together a little. Maybe that's just as important, too. You understand?"

"I want to set up an appointment with Mr. Walker so that you can talk to him directly."

"Would it do any good, do you think?"

"What do you mean?"

"What will he tell me?"

"He'll tell you what David needs to do to pass his class."

"Does David not know that? Is Walker keeping it a secret?"

"Mr. Bredesen."

"Charlie."

"It's quite obvious that David hasn't been doing his homework." She shuffled through a few papers. "His attendence has fallen off too. He's tardy to class."

"He doesn't sound interested."

"Nevertheless, he has an obligation to go."

He liked listening to her. Her voice was sweet and melodic with just a trace of Southern drawl that education couldn't remove. It wasn't at all nigger. Nigger irritated him because it always seemed contrived. How could anybody really talk nigger?

"He should go to class even though he's not interested and do the work though he's not interested and not be late even if he's not interested."

"I wouldn't put it like that."

"Are you interested?" he asked. "Vivian?"

"Do I like my work?"

"I guess so."

"Of course I like my work."

"That's good. You like working with young people."

"I enjoy it, yes."

He nodded and looked about. "You into running?" He pointed at the trophy.

"I was on the track team in college."

"Where was that?"

"Fresno State."

"Do you keep it up?"

"I still run."

"Where do you run?"

"I usually run around the track here in the late afternoon when everyone is gone, even the football team."

"People have been telling me I should get into running."

"It's good for you," she said. "It helps your disposition."

"Is that why you do it?"

"It clears your head," she replied.

"Is your head cluttered?"

"Isn't everyone's?"

"I guess that would mean David too, then."

She turned to look out the window. "I really think it's best for you to talk to Mr. Walker. I'll make an appointment for you. It would be good if Mrs. Bredesen could come too. The more concern shown for David the better. Don't you think?"

"Did I say something wrong?"

She dropped her eyes and her lower lip trembled. In fact, she had been struggling with it since he sat down.

"Really, I wanted to leave early today, Mr. Bredesen. I'm under some strain. Things have not been going too well the last few days. I only stayed at your wife's insistence."

"I'm sorry," he said. "I didn't want to come either."

"It's my job."

"I guess it's mine, too."

She stood up. He caught the strong scent of perfume. It was pungent and made him think of a room with no windows and all the lights off.

"Are you ill?" he asked.

"No, I don't think so."

The chairs faced each other, and they stood for an awkward moment. He was trying to determine which way to move, and as he figured it out and took a step, she ran right into him and both of her breasts, one after the other, slid across his arm.

"I'm sorry," he said.

He sat down.

He stared at the brass figure of the runner on the desk. The figure was wearing shorts and a halter top and there were two protrusions for breasts and the legs were a woman's legs all right, tapered that way from the thigh to the ankle. Only one foot touched the pedestal. The other was arched back, and he could feel the veiled, metallic wind that blew the fabric against those breasts, and he imagined her running around the track after the football team had left.

"Damn," he said, and crossed his legs.

She came back into the room holding a log book.

"The sooner the better," she said.

"What?" he asked.

"We should make your appointment right away."

"All right," he said. "Could you be there?"

"You want me to come?"

"Oh, yes," he said.

"Well, then, today is Wednesday. This week looks fairly tied up. Could we go bright and early next week, say Monday? Mr. Walker has nothing scheduled for Monday. At three?"

"That will be fine," he said.

"We can meet in my office."

"Fine, fine."

She closed the book. "Now, I must be going."

"All right," he said.

She stood and waited. "Mr. Bredesen."

"Could I just sit a moment?" he asked. "You go on ahead. I need to sit a moment, please."

"You want to just sit here?"

61

"Only for a few moments, please. Stomach's a bit quesy. I have a doctor's appointment at four, in fact."

She looked at him.

"Leave the door open if you like," he said. "Go on. You go ahead and go. I'll be all right. And thank you about David." He tried to keep his eyes on her face, but they slipped to her breasts.

"Don't concern yourself. I'll talk to the doctor about it. Probably nerves. It's happened before. I'll be fine."

She took a step back and her breasts moved. He turned his face away and bent over a little.

"I guess it will be all right," she said.

"Damn," he whispered. Then he nodded and said, "Thank you, Vivian."

When he looked back, she was gone.

He uncrossed his legs. The hard-on was so severe that he was afraid to stand up. He glanced through the doorway. No one was around. He stood slowly and saw a round lump appear under the wool of his right thigh. He put his hand into his pants and straightened himself against the zipper.

"Damn," he said.

He kept his back to the door and in a few minutes the blood returned to the rest of his body. He looked at the walls, where there were some certificates and photographs. The photographs were mostly of students and Vivian Chalmers with students. One said Student Council and there were signatures. But a couple of pictures were of more interest. They showed women standing in tennis shoes, shorts and halter tops. There was Vivian with three other black women. In the other photo she was standing next to a white woman.

He bent to look more closely. There was something about the flat, straggly hair of the white womam. He looked carefully.

Jesus H. Christ, it was Ruth Danilow.

A doctor's office is a horrible place. Charlie had always thought so. He went in and there was a counter that reminded him of the luggage counter at a Greyhound Bus station. Behind the counter was a basketball team of women hunched over phones, file cabinets and computer terminals. He signed his name on a clipboard and sat down in a waiting room to the right.

It was a family practice and, with various trips for the children over the years, Marian's periodic sexual eclipse by female problems, his own bouts with pneumonia and flu, he had watched it grow from a two horse operation (Dr. Michaels and Dr. Flowers, both of whom were gone now, Dr. Michaels, his first doctor, to a bout with cancer, and Dr. Flowers, who had performed the vasectomy after Kelly's birth, to a lucrative practice in Hawaii) into the corporation it now was, with ten doctors, two labs and a pharmacy.

There were three other people seated in the room, an old man with a runny nose whose fingers shook, a middle-aged woman with furtive, crossed eyes and a high school kid wearing a turned around baseball cap. People in doctors' offices don't like to look at you or talk to you because they don't know why you're there, and Charlie was always glad for this. He picked up last month's issue of Field and Stream and found an article about fishing in Alaska. His brother and he had always meant to go to Alaska, and he was two pages into a description of hooking five pound Dolly Vardon in the watershed of Bristol Bay when the Filipino nurse began calling his name.

"And how are you today, Mr. Bredesen?" she sang.

"Fine, Valerie, I'm just fine, thank you. Nothing's wrong with me."

"It's just a check-up, isn't it?" the nurse said, with a trace of accent. "We have to take your weight first."

He peeled off his coat and wished he could change the wingtips for Japanese thongs. Actually, it would really be fair only in his shorts. He looked at her as if to suggest that he could remove his trousers, but she was already playing with the weight on the cross bar, so he stepped onto the scales. She moved the weight to the right, then she moved it some more.

"Two twenty-six," she said.

He grinned foolishly, as though she had just caught him in the toilet. Christ, that was a good twenty pounds from what it should be for his height. He put his hand to his stomach. His stomach was over the rim of his belt.

"Now if you'll come with me," she said. "Doctor will be right with you."

It was a lie. The doctor wouldn't be right with him at all. She led him into an eight-by-eight room, told him to roll up his sleeves and closed the door as she went out.

There was a raised, cushioned table about the size of the air mattress he put under his sleeping bag. The table was covered with butcher paper. There was a stool next to the blood pressure apparatus on the wall, a tiny counter with a sink. The rest of the room was bare.

He sat on the air mattress and drew a deep breath. Someone at work had said that if you took a deep breath, held it for five seconds and let it out slowly, it would relax you. He took another breath and heard his heart beating. He let the air go.

This was the part he hated most, the part he truly hated. Seated in a tiny vestibule in the doctor's office, without even a porthole to see through, he could only imagine the worst. He hadn't made out a will. There was unfinished business with the family. And Alaska. He needed to go to Alaska. He heard voices in the hallway. Footsteps hurried by. In a sinking ship, he was going down alone.

The door opened and the nurse came in.

"All right, now come over here, Mr. Bredesen, and let's take that blood pressure."

He sat on the stool and she attached a wide rubber band to his arm. Then she smiled and propped his hand palm up against her hip. She pumped something with her right hand and he felt the band tighten. Sitting there, his arm imprisoned against her side, the pressure tightening just a little more, his eyes fixed upon hers as she watched the dial on the wall, he experienced the oddest sensation of pleasure.

He felt the pulse in his arm, the pressure let go, she pumped it up again, it went down again and she said, "160 over 102," and he realized he had been talking all the while.

"Is that OK?" he asked.

"Let's take the other arm," she said.

He turned a little. The same thing happened again. He could feel the bone in her hip.

"Don't talk this time," she said. "Talking increases heart activity."

In the quiet there was the squish-squishing of the bulb. As she turned, he heard the starch in her uniform. She coughed and he smelled garlic.

"162 over 101," she said.

He grinned. "That's OK, I'll bet?"

"The doctor will be right in, Mr. Bredesen."

"Charlie," he said.

"Doctor will be with you in a moment. You can roll down your sleeves now."

She went out.

"Bitch."

It wasn't all right. He didn't know anything about medicine. He was stupid about disease. He had thought herpes was just like clap and you could get AIDS from a water glass, but he knew 160 over 102 was too high. It said so on the machines in the supermarket.

He waited alone for what seemed an unconscionable number of minutes. He had time to sweat and then to stop sweating and become angry, and then the doctor walked in.

Jeffrey Keh didn't look like a doctor. He looked like a cook at the Mandarin Restaurant on West 24th. He wore a pair of flannel slacks, a print shirt and mailman shoes. He was balding. As he entered the room, he lit a cigarette.

"How you doing, Charlie?" he said, extending his hand. "Long time, no see."

"I guess I should have a checkup," Charlie said.

"Good boy."

Keh peered at some notes attached to a clipboard.

"How's business?" the doctor said. "Get up on the table, will you, and take off your shirt."

Charlie obeyed. It always seemed so important to obey when he was in this room. "Business is fine," Charlie said.

"That's good," Keh said.

His shirt off, his chest and stomach skin white and unused in contrast to the color of his forearms, Charlie felt like a beef in a slaughter house suddenly given the chance to think. There was a finality about such nakedness.

"How about you, Jeff?" He called the doctor by his first name and the same with his mechanic and his insurance man. They wouldn't cheat you maybe if you used their first name, and it made their information user friendly.

"I'm doing fine," the doctor said. "The practice couldn't be better. Just returned from Maui with the kids and my girlfriend. You still married, Charlie?"

"Yes."

"To your first wife?"

"The same one."

"That's good. That's good. The family is very important. My first wife and I just couldn't make it, you see. It's the personal thing that's given me the trouble. Bringing the work and the marriage together. You see what I mean? But I have hopes. I have hopes."

"You serious about this one?" Charlie asked.

"Why not? It looks good. And I enjoy being married. Some guys need to be married, and I enjoy it. I miss it."

All the while this was going on, the doctor circled him, tapping on his chest, tapping his back, checking his reflexes.

"Hold out your hands," he said.

Charlie held his hands out, and the doctor pulled at the tips of his fingers one by one.

"Feel anything?"

"No," Charlie said.

"Good, good. Take off your shoes and socks." He pulled at his toes. "Good," he said.

Keh produced a small Sony tape recorder and repeated his findings into the mouthpiece. Charlie imagined a secretary transcribing his life's history.

"Are you on any medication?" Keh asked.

"No."

"Any dizziness?"

"No."

"Any history of family illness?"

"Not that I know of," Charlie said.

"Is your father alive?"

Charlie looked at the wall. "No."

"What did he die of?"

"Heart attack."

"Have you experienced chest pains or shortness of breath?"

"No," said Charlie.

"Ever have trouble sleeping?"

"No."

"Headaches or any other pain?"

"No."

"Rashes?"

"No."

"Do you smoke or drink to excess?"

"I smoke some," Charlie said. "How much drinking is excess?"

"More than just socially, a drink or two."

"I wouldn't say so," Charlie replied.

Keh was making notes on his clipboard.

"Are your stools all right?"

"What do you mean?"

"You have no difficulty taking a shit?"

"Shitting is easy," Charlie grinned.

"Take off your trousers and shorts."

Charlie removed the rest of his clothes and stood flatfooted on the vinyl floor. The doctor took a step and placed his fingers under Charlie's scrotum. Charlie felt the doctor's fingers move. "Now cough," the doctor said. Charlie coughed. "Again." Charlie coughed and the doctor said, "Fine, fine."

Then Keh went to the cabinet and removed a small cardboard box. He took out a thin latex glove and pulled it over his right hand.

"The family is a big thing with us orientals," he said. "But I just couldn't keep the personal and the public thing on the same track. You have no problem with that?"

Charlie shook his head.

"Bend over."

Charlie turned away and the doctor placed his free hand on the small of his back.

"I studied philosophy in college," Keh said, "and psychology and anthropology. They were my first loves after medicine. None of that helped. Not even tradition helped. My children it doesn't bother so much as it bothers me. Half their friends' parents are divorced. But me it bothers, having to choose between my love of medicine and a wife. Wives often don't understand. Do you think?"

Charlie felt the doctor's finger circling in his asshole. It was a deep, pleasurable feeling and the closest he would ever come to being homosexual, but he was sorry when it was over.

"Here," the doctor said, handing him a moist napkin. Charlie looked puzzled. "Wipe," Keh said. "Get dressed. I'll be back in a moment." He pulled off the rubber glove, washed his hands and left the room.

Charlie noticed that there was no music in the room. Outside in the waiting room there was music, but in here there were only the muffled sounds from the corridor. There was no sky and he felt a need to see sky. He felt the need to hear voices and laughter. All of this had only one purpose, to measure how close he was to death. There was nothing for his imagination to get hold of. He found himself reading the names on the appliances and counting the cracks in the floor.

The doctor returned.

"Well," Keh said, "let's talk about that blood pressure. It's a bit high, you know."

"I guess it is," Charlie said.

"You have much stress at work?"

"No, I don't think so."

"Not tense or under pressure."

"Not any more than usual."

"Maybe something's going on you don't know about."

Charlie said nothing.

"Do you exercise regularly?"

"Play golf fairly often."

"You don't do any regular walking or running or anything like that?"

"No."

"Well, I can give you a prescription to get it down. We

want it down below ninety."

Charlie looked at him. "Isn't there something I can do myself? I've heard that once you get on that crap, you have to stay on it."

The doctor seemed impressed. "You want to try to lose weight and get into a regular exercise program?"

"Well, sure. Of course."

"That's not the easy way. The easy way is for me to give you a prescription."

"I don't want medicine, Jeff, if I don't need medicine."

"All right," the doctor said, lighting a cigarette. "I'll give you six months. Lose twelve pounds and get into walking or running at least three times a week. It doesn't make any difference how long or hard you exercise. Just get that heart rate up and keep it up for thirty minutes or so at least three times a week. Regularly. Can you do it?"

"Sure. Sure I can."

"Then we'll see if the blood pressure is related to hypertension or lack of exercise and being overweight. Okay?"

"Sure. Okay."

"Come in for a blood pressure check the first of each month."

"Okay."

"Before you leave, get into the lab for a chest x-ray and an EKG. I also want a blood sample. Might as well make it a thorough exam."

"Preventive medicine, right?"

"It must be true in your profession as well."

"I guess so. Never thought of it that way, though."

"By the way, you ever have any pain in your testicles?"

"No. Why do you ask that?"

"One hangs considerably lower than the other."

"Well, I'm right handed." He tried to laugh.

"It's true that many of us have one testicle hanging lower than the other; however, yours is exceptional. Ever have an accident?"

"When I was a kid, I ran into a lawn faucet. Full blast. Knocked me on my can. I almost couldn't breathe."

"That could explain it. You let me know if you ever start experiencing any kind of pain there, will you?"

"Jeff," he grinned, "I suffer there already more than you'll ever know."

The doctor smiled.

Charlie took the other tests in a state of reprieve, but before he left the office, he went into the waiting room and lifted the copy of Field and Stream.

CHAPTER FIVE

The old woman's head was pressed into the pillow. Charlie raised his eyes. Through the third story window he could see the parking lot below and the wind blowing the tops of the cypress trees across Ygnacio Valley Road. He went out into the corridor.

Against the wall was a wheelchair and in it was a man with snow white hair wearing a plaid flannel robe. He was waiting for a shove and in the meantime pushed at the arms of the chair with his bony, blue-veined hands, trying to stand. The male nurse attending him was twenty paces up the corridor at the IC center talking to a candy striper.

Charlie watched this Methuselah, who was straining so hard now that the cords on his neck were distended. He thought about helping, yet wasn't sure just what he should do. The old man began to paw at the wheels of the chair, but they had been locked, and in desperation he hunched his body forward in an attempt to overcome inertia. Charlie felt a little desperate.

"What the hell's going on here?" he said. "What in the hell am I doing? I don't want to be here. I don't have any obligation to be here."

73

The old man heard the voice and turned his scrawny neck. His mouth made little opening and closing motions, and the panic in his eyes led Charlie to think he was having some kind of attack. The geezer hunched and hunched and his eyes narrowed in pain, and then Charlie understood. The old boy had to pee. He just wanted to get to the head, that was all. His whole body was struggling for the dignity of taking a leak in private, while the sonofabitch who was supposed to watch him was off finger-fucking a blond volunteer worker. Charlie made a move toward the chair, but it was too late. Drops began trickling to the polished floor. The old man's eyes filled with tears.

Charlie walked to the window at the end of the corridor. He could see Mt. Diablo. It rose in the distance and made the rooftops and manicured trees of the town look like the debris at the bottom of an aquarium.

David came out of the room.

"Is Maju going to die, Dad?"

Charlie turned. The acne was fierce at the corners of the boy's mouth and on his forehead. The welling of anger and frustration that always surfaced when he regarded the face was not present at the moment. Even the blemishes had a kind of appropriate shyness. Maybe it was that something genuine was finally there in the world. The expression was not pulled back, and the thought occurred to Charlie that if they had spent their time talking about death and courage and hope instead of grades, drugs and expectations, some love might have grown between them, and they would not have become parent and child but father and son.

"I don't know," Charlie said. "It doesn't look so good. She's pretty sick and all."

"The doctor and Mom are talking."

"Are they?"

"Mom's crying."

74

He wanted to put his arm around the boy. He thought, if he could put his arm around the boy.

"She just lays there and doesn't open her eyes. I can't tell if she's sleeping or not."

"It's a tough thing. We'll all just have to do our best."

"I wonder if she'll even wake up," David said.

"Well, it's tough. She's had a good life, whatever."

He felt weak and foolish. Nothing had prepared him to face death with a son. There was some deep, momentous possibility here, but he was trapped behind a membrane and couldn't break through.

"Maybe we should go back now," he said.

They walked up the corridor. The old man in the wheelchair was gone and the floor had been mopped. At the IC center nurses were chatting and laughing. He glanced into a doorway. Something made of bone and skin was lying on a bed with a tube in its nose, and someone was sitting there watching television.

Inside his mother-in-law's room, Charlie took one look and turned away. Kelly was kneeling beside the bed and he heard God this and God that, forgive this and forgive that. Marian was sitting in a chair, her face pale and empty.

Charlie stood beside the chair so that he would not have to look at his wife. The thought that, at the end, there was nothing to do left him desperate. It seemed more reasonable to jump out the window than to wait like this.

He touched Marian's shoulder. She did not move. He left his hand there awhile and then put it into his pocket.

David stood at the foot of the bed staring at his grandmother, whose only sign of life was the blanket slowly rising and falling across her chest. Nothing in the slaughter and butchery the boy witnessed at the movies downtown could hold a switchblade or a laser to the quiet violence of Maju's dying.

Charlie listened for his heart. Somehow that mechanism's struggle to generate the force needed to send the blood to the edges of his toes and fingers had been lessened, or increased, which was it? The risk of crossing the street against a red light or of disconnecting a seatbelt had come into his body. His heart, his very own heart, might, at any time, be the instrument of his destruction.

"Amen," he heard his daughter say and was startled to find that ten minutes had elapsed. He looked at Marian. She was pushing at her breasts with a thumb and forefinger. He went out into the hall.

* * *

Change was in the air. Charlie had smelled it long before the Eisner Corp merger had been put into the oven.

You could smell it in the bars and grilles along Montgomery and Post, where people like himself lingered over gin fizzes and vodka tonics to talk of "enhancing the content of work" and "mutuality in labor relations." Catch words were as plentiful as green olives at the bottoms of martini glasses. A guy named Hodgkins, a systems manager for Echo Electronics whom he knew solely because he also liked Pilsner Urquel and ordered it often enough for Charlie to introduce himself one day, talked about "actuality thinking" and overcoming the "flat earth values" that inhibitted "creative imaging." Angela Tyson, about whom he had once entertained some acute sexual fantasies, but whose otherworldly tone had put him off, spoke in glowing terms about something she called "leadership esteem" and then broke into a few bars of *My Way*. He heard the phrase "unitive consciousness" from Lou Fargo of Forsman Burton, and Harley Barron asked him if he had tried transactional anaylsis. Jeanne Hume's favorite word was "nesting," and a company wasn't a company anymore, it was a "culture."

Company or culture, it was all bullshit to Charlie's

thinking. Business was business, and the bottom line was always money. "What are we running scared for?" he said coming off the bridge at Fremont Street that morning. "There are a bunch of guys getting rich out there because everybody needs his mother."

Even Janet looked at him differently when he stopped at her desk.

"Mr. Carpenter wants to see you," she said.

"Right away?"

"Right away. And congratulations."

"What for?"

"The promotion, of course."

"I haven't been promoted yet."

"That's not what I hear."

"I'm just one of many," he said. "I'm sure someone else is more worthy." He grinned.

"Go on," she said. "You're the best kid on the block. No problem."

He laughed. "I wish I had your confidence."

"Just remember where you heard it," she said.

He cocked his head. He liked her. She had an OK body but a lousy face that remined him of Mrs. O'Reilly, who had been den mother for a time to the boys of the old Phi Tau house at Berkeley. Mrs. O'Reilly's face looked like kneaded bread dough, lumpy and soft, but pleasantly natural, a face you could depend on.

"By the way," she asked, "how's the zipper holding up?"

"Fine," he said, "just fine. You do good work. You ought to get married and raise a family."

"Recommend somebody," she said.

He walked into the office. The copy of the Chron was still on the desk. He picked it up and read the story again. Then he went over to the window.

The bay was filled with light. The color of the water was

so blue that he felt he had just broken through to it out of a cover of cloud. There seemed to be nothing alive out there today. A few cargo vessels were anchored beyond Yerba Buena. There were no sailboats. The traffic moved along the bridge, but the pattern never varied, so that the cars were part of the span, like the girders and the spires.

Charlie took a deep breath.

When he had first moved into the room some years back, he kept the door open to Janet's office. He rather liked the tap tapping of her machines and the telephone going and there were people. He even enjoyed the hum of business leaking in from the cubicles beyond.

But he had been younger then. What was it, seven, eight years? "It wasn't all that long ago," he said, staring at the bay. "I've been with the company fifteen years, so it isn't that long ago."

He was not fond of solitude. Except for those moments in the BMW or those intervals along the trout streams in Montana when he moved out of sight from his brother, being alone for any period of time had the quality of waiting for an echo.

Yet, of late, he had taken to closing the door and he wasn't sure why. It had to do with a feeling, but he couldn't say for certain what it was. Sometimes it felt like anger and sometimes like a kind of cynicism and sometimes almost a despair, though that seemed a bit too much. He couldn't remember when it had begun to contaminate his spirit, but he had closed the door and turned the desk around so that his back was to the window.

It was like putting on weight. You just got on the scale one day and found yourself twenty pounds over, and then you remembered that after college you had been a thirty-four but now you were a thirty-eight, and you might as well throw the old jackets away, you were never going to lose the weight.

There was just too much crap you had to swallow to ever get slim again.

Charlie buttoned his coat and straightened his tie. Against the light from the bay he could see the reflection of his face upon the window pane, as in a transparency. The face was full of blue water, and the listless movement of the sea was in the eyes. He turned away and left the room.

"Janet," he said, stopping beside her desk, "I want you to check something."

She looked up, smiling. "You're the boss."

"I want you to call the Chron or maybe the city health department. Ask about a Ruth Danilow. See if you can find out where she lived. The kinds of things she was involved in. People. You know. Get some names. Whatever you can. But keep it to yourself. This is nobody else's business."

"You've got it," she said.

"I'm going up to see Carpenter."

"Ruth Danilow. That name's familiar. Wasn't she the gal who did a swan dive off. . .?"

He raised a finger to his lips and strode away.

Entering Carpenter's office alone had always disconcerted him a little. It wasn't the man so much. Carpenter himself was rather nondescript. He compensated for a plain, bland face and square frame with those expensive suits from Merriwether's, but his blockish body might better be adorned by a manufacturer of packing cases. His mind was unimaginative, yet possessed of a tremendous curiousity about how things worked, rather like the mind of a mechanic. One afternoon in those days when he had been reckless with Arleen Boggiano, Charlie had agreed to meet her down in the supply room, only to find Carpenter there, his shirt sleeves rolled up, repairing a ditto machine.

It was organizational talent that Carpenter possessed. He gathered men and women about him, gave them authority and read shop manuals between meetings. His hunger to understand the workings of gears and valves and rollers gave him the power to fix the movements of people among subsidiaries and franchises. The right person in the right place doing the right job, that was his credo. All you had to do was pull those factors together, and Carpenter did so remarkably well.

Maybe it was that beyond this office there was no place to go. Charlie came into the room and there was Carpenter, standing by the window, and this was it. If you aspired to success, if you wanted to go somewhere in the company, this was as high as you could go. There was a limit to ambition, then, no matter how strong the desire or greed. Everything stopped somewhere. Looking at Carpenter was like looking at the end of life.

"Come on over here, kid," he said.

Charlie walked to the window.

"Have you ever counted the vertical cables on that goddamn bridge?"

He looked. "No, sir, I haven't."

"When I was a boy, I was always fascinated by things like that. You know, how many steps up to the attic or how many spokes on the wheel of my bicycle or how many drops in a glass of water. I was always measuring stuff. Some day I'm going to drive across that goddamn bridge and count every one of those cables."

Charlie did not say anything. Carpenter put his hands behind his back.

"The old man wants you for the job, kid."

"What?" he said.

"We're making the motions to keep folks happy. You know how that goes."

Charlie looked through the windows.

"Once the merger is completely finalized, we're going to

move the whole damned operation from the American over to the New York Exchange. Two hundred million gross in three years, easy. We'll change the name of the company. A whole new image. A new view, Charlie. There are going to be other acquisitions. Other opportunities." Carpenter turned enough of his face so that Charlie could see his expression. "So don't blow it, kid. I need someone I can trust, you understand? I don't need Eisner people, and you know how that old sonofabitch is. Once he gets his mind on something, he's like a pit bull. You'd have to shoot the bastard to get him off."

"Blow it? What blow it?" Charlie said. He was dumbfounded, staring out the window.

"You don't seem too excited," Carpenter said. "It doesn't come as a surprise to you?"

"I don't know what you mean, blow it."

"Well, I like self-confidence. You did a hell of a job with the old man and he appreciates it. He wants you there. Quite frankly, I think he's pretty pissed off at his own people, though Lord knows why. So congratulations are in order but keep it mum, not a word to anyone, absolutely anyone, including Marian, until it's all signed and official. Comprende?" Carpenter put his hand on Charlie's shoulder and they were both looking through the window.

"I don't understand blow it," Charlie said.

"The remark you made."

"Remark. What remark?"

"About that nut who went off the bridge. He collared me after the meeting and wanted to know what you meant by asking him about the nut who killed herself. All the color was out of his face."

Charlie was looking at the water beneath the bridge.

"Why?" he asked.

"I don't know why and it doesn't make any difference, does it? He's a queer old bird. He's queer for female activists.

81

He had a daughter once."

"What do you mean?"

"Well, he has a daughter, I should say. Only they don't get along. I don't think they've talked in years. She tries to save things. You know, whales, redwood trees, the ozone, babies. He hates those damned women who part their hair down the middle and don't wear bras. His daughter was up in Oregon for awhile with that Hindu guru what's-his-name. The guy with all the Rolls Royces. Got her head turned around. I don't think he knows where she is now. Maybe what you said set him off. It was completly an accident, of course. But maybe he'd like to see all these radical types go off a bridge."

"I asked about Ruth Danilow. I didn't ask about his daughter."

"I'm just trying to make it easy, kid. You understand."

"Who the hell is Ruth Danilow?"

"That's none of your business."

Charlie turned to look at him. Carpenter's eyes were wide and steady and he wet his lips.

"I saw her get out of her car and walk over to the side of the bridge. She just rolled over and was gone. She killed herself in front of me, and I've seen her in the Petrini's buying meat. I don't even know her. It was only a point of clarification. I stuck my fucking tongue out at her going up to the Caldecott, and she turns a dozen somersaults off the bridge in front of me. What the hell did she do?"

"Jesus Christ, you saw her take the dive?"

"I was right there," Charlie said. "Right behind her. What the hell did she do?"

"She didn't do anything, that's the point. And if she did, it wouldn't make any difference, see? It was just an unfortunate remark. That Eisner man's at fault. Phil Carey. The old man's nephew. Dumb sonofabitch. What can you do? The old man's queer, that's all. He's queer for whatever gets in the way of

82

free enterprise. Free enterprise built this country and he's one of the old breed. If he had it his way, he'd repeal the income tax, social security and the Taft Hartley Act. That's the name of the animal. It's all a mountain out of a molehill, but we have to live with it. You understand? Jesus Christ, you saw her dive."

"You're not making sense," Charlie said.

"I know. Maybe I'm talking too much. Probably should have kept my mouth shut. It was a one-shot deal and all, I suppose. But who knows how and when these things slip out, and a word to the wise, that's all, kid. I want you in that spot, but, Charlie, there are other able men in this firm. The whole issue is irrational. That's the point. That's what I'm trying to explain. He's queer for his own daughter. What do you expect? And I don't want something to happen out of carelessness. So don't mention Danilow's name again, comprende? and you've got the job."

Carpenter walked to the cabinet on the wall behind his desk and came back with a bottle and two glasses. He put the glasses on the desk and opened the bottle.

"How are Marian and the kids?"

"They're all right," Charlie said.

"Good. Good. Sometimes I think a fellow's family is all that counts in this world. It's the only thing that stays close, know what I mean? I've got three grandkids now. Greatest little kids you'd ever want to see. They do something for a fellow, give him back something. There's almost an innocence about it. You forget everything else when you're with them. Everything." He handed Charlie a glass and walked to the window. "You'll know someday when you have some of your own. When you're with them . . . I mean it's just you and them . . . it's as though you can go back again and you haven't made any mistakes because you're just too young for any of it to matter. It's just back at the beginning and you wish you could stay there with them and start all over again."

Charlie had the glass in his hand. There was a blue light in the room, and he imagined that it came from the sea. Carpenter was drinking and the light came up around him and Charlie thought maybe the man had just asked to die, and there he was over by the window drinking and getting ready.

* * *

When he returned to his office, Janet handed him a slip of paper.

"And there's a package for you on your desk," she said. "Special delivery."

"A package from whom?"

"Don't know. A man just brought it."

Charlie looked at the slip of paper. "Is this all you could get?"

"The Chron didn't have any more details and the health department was pretty tight lipped. All I could get was that she was a case worker at someplace called San Francisco Opportunity House. Unwed mothers. Rapes. Abortions. All the happy stuff. She was employed there for nearly seven years, and then suddenly, a week ago, she just up and quit."

"Was she in trouble?"

"I don't know. I couldn't get anything out of the gal at the clinic, but what I gather from between the lines is that it took them all pretty much by surprise."

"What do you mean?"

"Well, she just stopped coming in. That was that."

"I'll be damned," Charlie said.

"You going to let me in on it?"

"I wish I could," he said. "I don't even know what I'm in on myself. Did you find out where she lived?"

"They wouldn't tell me. But she was coming this way across the bridge, wasn't she? So you know it's in the East Bay."

"Brilliant, Mr. Holmes."

"Elementary, Dr. Watson."

"But where in the East Bay?"

"Do you have any clues?"

"I've seen her shopping at the Petrini's in Pleasant Hill, that's it."

"Look in the phone books for Pleasant Hill, Orinda, Lafayette and Walnut Creek. Have you tried that?"

"No. But I'll bet the number's unlisted."

"Well, then, you're screwed."

"No, I'm not. I have an idea."

"What idea?'

"Sam Wanamaker owes me a favor and he's a florist."

"So?"

"So some roses are going to arrive at Opportunity House from bereaved cousin Gertrude back in Kalamazoo."

"What is all this?" she asked, her hands on her hips.

"I wish I knew. But keep it under your hat. Your promotion's at stake too." And he winked.

Charlie went into the office. The package was lying on the desk. He tore off the paper and smiled. He had been wondering who the other candidates were. "Here's one of them."

Inside the package was a new pair of bib overalls.

* * *

It was lunch, but he spent it eating a Big Mac and riding in Sam Wanamaker's van to the clinic on South MacDougall. He liked it in the van. The flowers, portioned out neatly in special racks, smelled heavy and sweet. He often walked by the street vendors in Union Square or at the wharf and stopped to look at the flowers stuck into the five gallon cans, but he had never bought any. He liked flowers and liked them in a house in the summer, but the roses, wrapped neatly in green cellophane at his feet, were the first flowers he had bought in twenty years.

When they got to the clinic, he told the driver, whose name was Tony, to wait in the van. Wearing a green apron, Charlie carried the roses into the stucco building.

There was a woman in a white smock standing behind a counter. A few wooden benches like the benches in an old bus station lined the floor before the counter. There was a hallway and doors with brass knobs. Two Mexican women were seated on one of the benches when he entered. One of the women, the young one, was holding a baby and crooning. A boy, who looked no older than sixteen and was obviously the husband, sat opposite the women staring at the floor. When the girl with the baby saw the flowers, she burst into tears. The boy got up and walked to a window.

He stepped to the counter and the woman in the white smock, who paid no attention to the girl who was crying, said, "Oh, how lovely."

"Delivery," Charlie said.

"Long stemmed roses," the woman, who had buck teeth, said. "Oh, how I wish it was me."

"Special delivery," Charlie said.

"Who are they for?"

Charlie looked at the card.

"A Ruth Danilow," he said.

"Oh, my," the woman said. "That's so awful. I mean, she doesn't work here any more. She's dead, I mean."

"That's why we brought the flowers. From a relative back East. Last address she had. The lady moved or something. Would you have the new address? Hate to have the flowers go to waste. Expensive, you know."

"Well, we just can't give out that information."

"It's a relative," Charlie said. "A blood relative. "

"The information is confidential." The woman's eyes went to a small card file on her desk. "I just couldn't give it out."

"It's a relative," Charlie said. "Somebody who loved her very much."

"Oh, my," the woman said. "I'll have to talk to my supervisor about this. If you'll wait here, please."

The woman jumped up from behind the desk and hurried down the hall. Charlie went around the counter and opened the file. He found the card with Danilow's name and put it into his pocket. He took the dozen roses to the Mexican girl and dropped them into her lap. Then he ran out the door.

* * *

The family rarely ate together, even on Sunday. By noon Marian was usually too inebriated to cook. He enjoyed golf in the afternoon, and, after a hand or two of gin rummy, a few table snacks and drinks, he definitely had no appetite. Dave was in some kid's garage twanging his guitar and fantasizing about how the band they would form would one day pack the Concord Pavillion. Kelly toted her leather bound Bible and some pamphlets concerning the benefits of prayer to a friend's bedroom, where they read passages from Matthew or Mark, drank diet Pepsi and whispered about the second coming of Christ.

It was just as well. Dinner was a time when expectations revived. Issues, once thought dead and buried, found a resurrection of sorts on the wings of recent failure. Arguments flared, shouts and reprimands. Someone would leave the table. Or a silence fell, punctuated by the clink of silverware. Or the television came on, bathing their faces in a holy blue light that saved them from each other.

This seemed somehow natural to Charlie, and yet it always saddened him. Then later he would wander into the kitchen, and perhaps David would be there, putting a tray into the microwave, or maybe Marian was at the formica table eating something with lettuce and croutons. Or Kelly would be fumbling inside the refrigerator looking for the yogurt or cottage cheese. It was now that pleasantries were exchanged. A hand might touch a shoulder. He might tousle someone's hair. There might be laughter.

More often than not forgiveness had not come, and he would find a half-eaten bag of French fries or a styrofoam carton from Wendy's or McDonald's or tiny, unused tubs of hot sauce or honey. He would sit down alone with the Monterey Jack, mayonaisse and wheat bread, and as he ate the sandwich, he listened to the house give up its sounds of loneliness.

But something in the hospital room with Maju had chilled them, and this Sunday they drew together around the roast beef for warmth.

Kelly was wearing the white cashmere sweater that showed off her chest and reminded him of Christmas. When he passed her the mashed potatoes, she smiled shyly, and he wondered if any of the boys whose names he heard from her lips over the telephone or saw scrawled into her yearbooks had ever fondled those breasts.

David had on a sweatshirt advertising Corona Beer, and his face was empty and indifferent. Marian sat at the other end of the table. Her bland, toothless grin and slightly exaggerated gestures let him know that she had had at least one drink too many.

When all the dishes had been passed and the plates were full and steaming, Kelly turned to him. "Daddy?" she said quietly.

"What is it, Kitten?"

"Could we say grace, please?"

"Grace?"

"Please," she said.

He looked at Marian, who bobbed her head like a bird. He was embarrassed. They had stopped all that years ago. There had been a time when they had attended church, fairly regularly, come to think of it. But that had only been out of a vague sense of moral obligation toward young souls coming into an evil world. By the time Kelly had hit the third grade, they had cut back to the holidays and an occasional visit from his mother.

There had been a time in his own youth when he had been religious. There was something about Catholicism and boyhood that went together. Perhaps it was the incense or the pagentry or that mass was still in Latin. An urgency lay behind the altar and the Stations of the Cross, and he went sometimes into the church alone to visit it. He thought it was God, but when he got older and discovered girls, he knew what it was and then he didn't go anymore.

David had already rolled a ball of roast beef into one cheek. He stopped chewing and looked at his sister with malevolent spite.

"We used to say it," Kelly said, "when I was little. Remember?"

"Sure," he said. "Sure. Well."

"We should start thanking God again for what we have."

He looked at the plate of food. That such abundance might be the work of an unseen hand astonished him.

"I guess it would be OK," he said. "Marian?"

"Of course it's OK. It's a fine idea. Kelly, it's just fine that you're so concerned about such things. We're so proud of you. We could all do with a little more piety."

He glared at Marian.

"Do you want to say it, Dad?"

"No, that's all right"

"Mom?"

"Oh, I don't think so, dear. It's such a marvelous idea. Wouldn't you like to do it?"

David swallowed the lump of food and set his fork down.

Kelly bent her head.

"Bless us, O Lord, for these gifts, which we are about to receive through thy bounty, from Jesus Christ, our Lord. And we pray thee to guide us in thy love and to show the world the way out of its wickedness and fear and turn everyone back to thy mercy and forgiveness and help the world to see that all of us are sacred and precious and that none of us should be thrown aside, for all of us are in thy image and in thy hands and without thy love we are nothing. Amen."

Charlie's heart was a drum and he didn't like that. He felt guilty and he liked that even less. He glanced at his son, whose face had an odd distance, and wondered why David had never wanted to go fishing over the years or to play golf. He had asked the boy often, but David showed no interest. He'd rather stay in his room, watch the television and, later, play his guitar or go out with his friends.

Marian's eyes were glassy and he knew damned well she was remembering something sentimental.

"That was very nice, Kelly," she said. "Those were marvelous words."

David picked up his knife. "Mom, is there any milk?"

"Of course, dear." She stood and moved toward the kitchen.

Charlie looked at his two children and then brushed his fork off the table.

"Oh, oh," he laughed. "Now I'll have to get a clean one."

He went into the kitchen.

"What is all this?" he said.

"All what?" Marian said, pulling a half gallon of milk from the refrigerator.

"It's getting too much, that's what. First it's nerds with polished hair and cheap copies of the New Testament filling the house. Then it's praying around a flag pole at school and now grace at dinner. I'm not going to have prayers over my food every goddamned time we sit down to eat, thank you."

"Why don't you relax?" she said.

"She's getting too much into this religion stuff. It's all she talks about."

"So what? What difference does it make? She's gotten a little carried away, that's all. Is that so bad? You ought to be pleased someone in this family has a little sense of morality."

"What the hell's that supposed to mean?"

"It doesn't mean anything." She took a pitcher from the cupboard next to the sink. "Why don't you be a little understanding?"

He pulled back a drawer and picked out a fork. "I suppose you're going to tell me now she's become one of those born again characters."

"What if she has?"

"Has she?"

"How the hell do I know? I don't talk to her about it. She has a mind of her own. I'm not going to tell her how to use it."

"But she's using it on the rest of us. Can't you talk to her, turn her around or some damned thing?"

"What am I supposed to say? Don't believe in God, Kelly. Be an atheist, like your father."

"That's chickenshit."

"Well, you don't believe in God."

"What's that got to do with anything?"

"Do you?"

"Do you?"

"Of course I do. I believe there's something out there. Some force or something."

"Oh, swell. So here we are arguing metaphysics in the kitchen while our dinner gets cold in the dining room. Let her believe anything she wants. I just don't want her draping it all around us. You're her mother, for chrissake. You're both the

91

same sex. You ought to be able to sit down and talk to her."

"Fine," she said, "fine." She dropped the empty carton into the trash compacter and turned it on. "Then I'll tell you what you do, Charlie. You sit down with your son and ask him why he's fucking up in school. You turn him around. Okay?"

"I'll talk to him."

"Fine. Talk to him."

"I said I would."

She let the compactor run. "What you have to understand is that Kelly lost Cindy Martin in an automobile accident two months ago and now there's this business with her grandmother. You know how close she is to Maju. She's frightened, that's all. When Mother gets better . . ."

Charlie turned the fork in his hands. Marian stared at the pitcher of milk.

"I don't want to talk anymore about it," she said. "We ought to leave things alone. Just leave them alone."

Charlie took a step toward her. Down at the bottom of the compactor a crushed rectangle of material was being formed no bigger than his hand.

"Maybe we ought to just be happy we have them," she said, still looking at the milk. "The world is so fucked up, just having them should be enough. We can't leave them alone. We worry them to death. No wonder they all want to kill themselves."

"They don't want to do that."

"I was reading an article in the paper the other day."

"That's not our kids." He stepped closer and touched her shoulder. "Our kids are OK."

"Then we ought to stop picking on them."

"Is that how you feel?"

"What do you mean?"

"Picked on."

"I'm not picked on. This kid's all right."

"Who said you weren't?"

"There's nothing wrong with me."

"That's a high five."

"So what if you're up for a big promotion. You earned it."

"So I did. And you're not jealous."

"Not me."

"Not even a a bit. After all, you've got a college degree."

"Just more money to spend."

"You could stay home."

"Fat chance."

"With all that money, you wouldn't have to work."

"I like to work."

"But you wouldn't have to."

"I need to."

"You don't need to."

"Catch me sitting home twiddling my goddamn thumbs while you conquer the world."

"We could go back to the old values."

"Bullshit."

"You could have my pipe and slippers waiting for me. We could go out to dinner in your new white Mercedes that I'd buy you. It would have a personalized license plate. Anything you wanted to say."

"Fuck you."

"You couldn't say that."

"Fuck me."

He put his hand on her ass. "You can't say that either."

"You can't do it."

"Is that a bet?"

The compactor made an odd settling noise. She switched it off and picked up the milk.

"I don't know."

"It's been two weeks. You know what they say."

"It's not the right season."

"C'mon. Spring training. Put your pussy where your mouth is."

"That's not my job." She was smiling.

"But I love the work."

"You hate your work."

"I wasn't supposed to tell you, so don't change the subject. We're talking about pussy."

"I don't care if you do become president."

"I don't care either."

"You hate your job."

"I know."

"Why do you go there if you hate it so much?"

"It amuses me. It's easier that way and the pay's good."

"You think we should cancel the appointment with David's counselor?"

"No, we should go."

"Maybe we're pushing him too hard."

"We'll go."

"We're making him fail."

"Bullshit. He fails on his own."

"I wish I'd never had him."

"C'mon. Cut that out. Are you going to play ball or not?"

"Play with your one ball?"

"The other one's there."

"You have to look close."

"It's hanging around. That's not what counts anyway."

"Your bat isn't heavy enough."

"C'mon, cut it out."

"You hit singles."

"Home runs. Long ball Charlie they call me."

"Pop fly Charlie."

"Over the center field fence and slow around the bases. C'mon, you love it."

"Do I get a corndog and a beer?"

"You get a Mercedes with a personalized license plate."

"Pop fly."

"Home run."

She set the milk on the counter.

"I'm scared."

"I know." He put his arms around her.

"I'm scared to even look at her."

"All right," he said.

"She's going to get better, isn't she?"

"Sure. Sure she is."

"The doctors don't tell you a fucking thing."

"What do they know?"

"How was your checkup?"

"I'm fine."

"Are you sure?"

"I'm fine. Why would I lie?"

"You wouldn't lie to me."

"No, I wouldn't lie to you."

"Everybody lies. That was one of Mother's favorite things. That's the only way we can be allowed to live. She always said so."

"She lied."

"You wouldn't lie to me."

"No, I wouldn't."

"I think doctors lie to make you feel better."

He didn't say anything.

"They make you feel better and then it's all over."

"Shhh," he said.

"Doctors are such fucking assholes."

"All right," he said. "All right."

He was holding her and then the door opened and Kelly came in.

"Mom, Dad, is anything wrong?"

"No, Kitten, everything's fine."

95

"How come you're taking so long?"

"We just got to talking."

"Everything's getting cold."

"C'mon," Charlie said. "Let's go eat roast beef."

It wasn't easy for Charlie being in the dining room with these people. He thought he loved them. Or believed he did. Hell, he did. But it was almost the way you are at a movie you've seen many times. You sit out there and up on the screen are these people you know so well, you know exactly what they're going to say or do next, you can even mouth the lines along with them, and there they go, but they're not you. You're the audience and after the performance you can leave, but Charlie didn't leave. He lived in the theater with them and watched the movie over and over. And that was love.

"Well, the gravy's cooled off," Marian said.

"That's all right," Charlie said. "We can make out. OK, kids?"

"Speaking of making out," Marian said.

Kelly giggled.

"Mom," David said.

"Well, tell your father," Marian said.

"Tell me what?"

"Dear, would you go put the gravy bowl into the microwave a few minutes."

"All right, Mom," Kelly said.

"Tell me what?" said Charlie.

"Your son has a girlfriend."

"What's new about that?"

"Tell him, David."

"Mom, it's no big deal. Jesus."

"This is serious," Marian grinned.

"Oh, how serious?"

"He's going steady with this one."

"Mom, people don't go steady anymore."

"Where do they go?" Charlie asked.

"They just go," said David.

"He's only known her two weeks. That's why we haven't seen her yet."

"Getting acquainted first," said Charlie.

"Funny," David said.

Kelly returned with the gravy and it went quickly around the table.

"That's how it is these days," Charlie continued. "People think with what's between their legs, not with what's between their ears. I hope you're taking care of things. We don't want to be paying to undo some accident around here."

"For chrissake, Dad."

"Your father is just kidding, dear," Marian said. "Aren't you, Charles?"

Charlie looked at his family. He grinned. "Sure," he said. "Kidding."

Kelly, who had held her head still over her plate, said, "There you go again."

"There I go again what?" Charlie said, mixing his peas in with a lump of mashed potatoes, the way he had done as a boy.

"You shouldn't talk like that, Daddy. You don't care. God wants you to care. You'll go to hell if you don't care."

Was this assumption his own daughter wished upon him an article of faith or cold, hard fact?

"Kelly," Marian said.

"Well, it's true, Mother. He just makes fun of everything. He doesn't take anything seriously."

"Tell him, little sister," David said.

"Oh, shut up," said Kelly. "You're just as bad. I just want to say a little grace at the dinner table and you make a big federal case out of it."

"Hey, you said grace, didn't you?"

97

"We ought to say thanks after everything. If it weren't for God, we wouldn't have anything."

"All right, Kelly," Charlie said.

"It's not all right. And it's not funny. It's perfectly understandable to me why people blow up those places."

"Blow up what places?" David said, in spite of himself.

"Those places where they have those operations."

"You're in favor of blowing up abortion clinics?" Charlie said. "Isn't that a bit hypocritical? I mean, violence in the name of stamping out violence."

"At least those people care about something. They care about life."

"Why don't we just drop it everybody," Marian said. "Would anybody like some more roast beef?"

"I care about life," Charlie said. He felt the back of his neck getting warm.

"Somebody's got to do something. There are women who are dying because of how they're keeping babies from being born."

"What are you talking about?" Charlie said. "What women?"

"I heard about it at church."

"Church? What church?"

Kelly looked about the table. "I joined a church. A lot of my friends at school belong, too."

"What church?"

"Boulevard Baptist."

"Marian, did you know about this?"

"I suspected something was happening. I think it's fine she cares so much."

"You were baptized Catholic," Charlie said.

"Catholics don't do anything," Kelly replied.

"What does that mean?"

"It doesn't mean anything."

"What's going on?" said Charlie.

"Nothing, Dad."

"If you were baptized a Catholic, you should stay a Catholic. If you're going to be anything, be a Catholic."

"I don't want to be a Catholic."

"Catholics don't believe in birth control."

"I know. But they don't do anything."

"Do? What's to do?"

Kelly frowned and pushed at her mashed potatoes with a fork.

"I want to do something," she said.

Charlie threw up his hands.

"For godssake, Kelly, don't you think most of this comes from the fact that Maju is dying?"

As soon as he said it, he wished he hadn't. A silence struck the room. It was the terrible. The unforgivable. The real.

"I'm sorry," he said. "I only meant . . ."

Kelly's face was as white as her sweater.

"You bastard," Marian said.

"I only meant," Charlie said.

Marian got up and switched on the television.

* * *

He was the first to arrive at the office. He sat in the chair where he had sat before and Vivian Chalmers said, "When David and Mrs. Bredesen get here, we'll go over to the vice-principal's office. It's a bit larger and we'll be more comfortable. Mr. Walker will meet us there."

"All right," Charlie said.

Driving across the bridge, he had been apprehensive about being in the same room with her again, but the plain brown suit she was wearing made it easier. That, and the picture with Ruth Danilow on the bookcase. There were a dozen questions, but he didn't know where to begin.

99

"How have you been?" he asked.

"I've been all right. But what about you? How's your stomach?"

"My what?"

"Your stomach. You were going to the doctor."

"Oh, that. It's OK. He wants me to lose weight. Exercise. The usual stuff."

"I see," she said.

"Running, maybe."

"That would be good."

"Well, jogging. Actually, I might just walk. I see a lot of guys just walking."

"Walking is good too, if you do it briskly and regularly."

"You run, though," he said, looking at the picture.

"It's more intense," she said.

"More intense?"

"It's more physical."

She glanced out the window, and he thought he saw a gleam in her eye. He liked her more.

"Does your husband run too?" he asked. Sometimes a bare finger didn't mean a damned thing.

"I don't have a husband."

"Oh," he said.

"I had one, but we're divorced."

Charlie looked out the window at some kids walking across the quad.

"Seems the way of things."

"You've been divorced?"

Charlie thought for a moment. "No," he replied.

"He wanted to stay home, drink beer and watch television while I went to work. One day he took a swing at me and I hit him with a lamp and that was that."

Charlie looked at her.

"He was a professional athlete, or thought he was.

100

Professional athletes don't have to do anything."

"Why are you telling me all this?"

"I don't know," she said. "Maybe I just want to tell somebody something. You just happen to be convenient." She tried to smile, and Charlie had to resist the urge to reach over and pat her thigh.

"You seemed a little upset the other day."

"I was. I've lost a good friend."

Charlie forced himself not to look at the photograph.

"Sorry," he said.

"It happens," she replied. "Life goes on. But nobody likes being kicked in the stomach."

"That's true."

"Have you been kicked?"

Charlie turned a few things over in his head. "Not lately," he said.

"Well, anyway, you don't want to hear about that. After all, I'm the counsel, aren't I?"

Charlie lowered his eyes. Actually, he would have liked to hear anything she had to tell him. He had not known many black women and had never made love to one, though there was that Stephanie in personnel a few years back, fresh out of school and hungry to get ahead and him just eager as hell to help, but she was caught stealing software and quit before anything came off between them.

"Counselors need counseling sometimes," he said. It was corny and stupid, but his heart was beating.

"I guess they do," she said, picking up a folder on the desk, for just at that moment David and Marian came into the room.

Charlie introduced his wife, and they all walked down the corridor and past fat and lean at the front desks. They went into another wing of the building. Vivian opened a door with a sign that read Dean Weldon, Vice-Principal.

It was a clean, uncluttered office. On the wall behind the desk were several rows of those cheap walnut frames that insignificant people feel compelled to fill with diplomas, certificates of membership and honoraria from the Boy Scouts and the PTA. A couple of potted plants, some student art work and a photograph of an innocuous, short-haired woman and two bland-faced kids standing next to a palm tree above a long, white beach. There was a small sofa against the wall next to the door and opposite the desk several vinyl-cushioned chairs. Sitting in one of the chairs was the sonofabitch who had pulled him away from Glen Miller. He stood up. He was wearing the same doubleknit pants.

"Mr. and Mrs. Bredesen," Vivian said, "I'd like you to meet Mr. Walker, David's English teacher."

Charlie made a move to extend his hand, but Walker sat down. Charlie put the hand into his pocket. Marian, David and he perched on the sofa. Vivian went behind the desk.

"Well, David," she said, "it seems we're still having problems with English. Is that right?"

David shrugged.

"Would you like to talk about it?"

Walker opened his briefcase and removed a small, brown record book. David stared at it.

"I dunno," he said.

"Is the work too hard for you?" she asked.

Walker thumbed through the book, found the right page and sat back. Charlie watched him.

"No," David said.

"You're able to understand it, you mean."

He nodded.

"It's not too hard and you can do the work, but you're failing the class. I'm afraid I don't understand, David."

"If I may," Walker said. He flipped a page. "In the last three weeks David has been tardy to class seven times. Two

102

of the tardies are three minutes in length, one is five and the other four are eight, ten, twelve and twenty minutes respectively. In addition, David is disruptive, inattentive and unprepared to do his assignments."

Walker looked at them, and Charlie hated him with a ferocity born of impotence and frustration. He felt something very far down. When he was small, there had been another room and someone else, only female; in fact, they had all been female, all the teachers in the school, and he had had that feeling of small and helpless and that fuckshit female over him with the answers and a face like this bastard, cold and held back, the power of the institution, the refuge of callousness and indifference pressed there like the stones of a building. Walker had a salt and pepper beard that he shaved carefully along the chin. The hair came out of his nose and the upper lip curled into it. The lower lip was soft, and when Walker stopped talking, the lips stayed parted just a little and reminded Charlie of the anus of a cow.

"Sounds to me as though he's not interested," he said.

"Say again."

"I said he may not be interested."

Walker's lips puckered. He brought his legs together. Charlie looked at Vivian. She shook her head.

"Do you like the class, David?" she asked.

David tilted his head.

"Well, do you or don't you?" Charlie said.

"It's all right."

"What do you mean, it's all right?"

"It's all right," David said.

Charlie looked at the teacher, whose eyes had narrowed with a satisfaction that something he had suspected all along had just been verified. "Have you tried to help him?" Charlie said.

"Of course," Walker said.

"How?"

Marian put her hand on Charlie's arm.

"Any of my students can get help anytime by coming in after school and talking to me. I encourage that. I also have a preparation period, period two. David could have come in then to see me."

"I have a class period two," David said.

"David, I told you I would give you an admit to your period-two class if you wanted to see me then."

"Mrs. MacGregor doesn't want me to."

"She's your period-two teacher?"

"Yeah."

"I would be happy to clear the time with her."

"But she still wouldn't like it."

"It would be excused, David."

"But she wouldn't like it. Then I'd be missing her class."

"Well, then, why haven't you come in after school?"

"I did come in."

"No, you didn't."

"You were gone. You always leave right after the last bell."

"I don't always do that, David."

"I came in twice and you weren't there."

"You should make an appointment with me."

"How can I make an appointment if you're not there?"

"In class, David, in class." Walker threw up his arms.

Charlie was staring at Vivian's breasts. They really were quite enormous. He wondered about the color of the nipples. They wouldn't be black, not like her skin. When he looked down at his hands resting on the arms of the chair, he was surprised to see that they had turned into fists.

"Well, then, we have a communication problem, don't we?" Vivian said.

"Say again," Walker declared.

"She says it's an English class and there's a problem in communication," Charlie said.

Marian sat forward. "Mr. Walker, what does David have to do right now to pass your class? It seems to me that's the important thing. Wouldn't you agree?"

Walker turned with a look that showed he had only just recognized her existence, and Charlie thought, you faggot sonofabitch.

"It's almost the end of the semester," the teacher said.

"What does that mean?" Charlie asked.

"There's not much time left, Mr. Bredesen. That's what it means."

"My son has been having trouble in your class and you're telling us it's too late?"

"I haven't said that, Mr. Bredesen. What I am saying is that there are standards. There are expectations. Everything just can't be done at the last minute in a hodgepodge. There is careful work that should have been completed right along. One thing builds upon another. I'm sure you can appreciate that. If we don't have standards, how can we expect to achieve excellence, and, quite frankly, Mr. Bredesen, I'm not interested in mediocrity, are you? Or just getting by? Is that the model we want to hold up for our children, that they should just get by? Quite frankly, in the world these days we can't afford to get by. Is that how you run your business?"

"Never you damned well mind how I run my business," Charlie said. "My business is not at issue here, yours is."

"I'm doing my job, Mr. Bredesen." Walker dropped his brown record book into the briefcase.

"If you were doing your job, my son wouldn't be failing."

"Say again," Walker replied. His eyes had narrowed, but his fat lips were trembling. He drew up against the back of the chair.

"I'll say again. What's the idea of failing my son when he

tried to come to you for help?"

"I told you about that."

"What you told me is that you split from school when the last bell goes off. How's any kid supposed to see you?"

"Mrs. Chalmers," Walker said.

Vivian stood up. Charlie stood up too. David sat staring at his father, a quirky little smile at the corners of his mouth.

"Perhaps it would be best to talk some other time. I'll speak to Mr. Walker. I'm sure he'll want to cooperate. No teacher is interested in failing students."

Walker was busy with his hands. "I sent a deficiency report home to you at the first sign of difficulty," he said. "I did not hear from you. Time went on and things got worse. I suggested to David that he speak to me after school. All he had to do was make an appointment. At the beginning of the school year I distribute a handout to my students with my grading policy and the tardy and absence policy of the school. The policies are all contained in the student handbook as well, and every student gets one of those at the beginning of each school year. My appointment policy is down there in black and white, and every student is given a copy of it. I review the policy with my students each year. Some students don't listen, that's quite apparent. I've been teaching for sixteen years, Mr. Bredesen, and some students like me and some students don't and, quite frankly, that's no concern of mine because I'm there to teach them English. That's my business, Mr. Bredesen, teaching them English, not being responsible for their conscience and morality, which are properly the business of the home. Quite frankly, I don't understand what parents want from education these days. They've shoveled everything off onto us, and these things are not our responsibility. Our responsibility is to teach. I do not think our society understands what it is doing to itself, but I am here to teach, Mr. Bredesen, and I do that

106

well. I am a good teacher. I was graduated with honors from San Francisco State. I have written articles for scholorly journals. I am here to teach Shakespeare and Dickens and Edgar Allan Poe. I am not here to raise children whose parents cannot raise them themselves. I am not a father or a mother. I teach English in this high school. Quite frankly, Mr. Bredesen, it's little enough, but it's what I do."

There was a long moment of silence, and Charlie remembered the only play by Shakespeare he had been required to read in high school. They had all taken parts. For awhile he had been Antony. He had tried to memorize the speech about honorable men, but he couldn't do it. It was too damned long, and anyway he couldn't get out of his mind the image of Caesar covered with stab wounds dead on the floor of the senate, so the teacher, old Mr. Humbarger, had let him read it from the book. Caesar, that was the guy who fascinated him, not Antony. But Caesar had been murdered, and here was this polyester sonofabitch sounding like something honorable.

Then David jumped up and pointed. "You said my report on Red Badge of Courage was stupid."

Charlie stared at David. That this person should be his son, that he, therefore, had certain obligations seemed ludicrous and unfair. Walker's face turned grey.

"I would never say anything like that to any student."

"You said it was stupid."

"I certainly did not."

"Someone is lying, then," Charlie said.

"Charlie," Marian gasped.

"Well, I think this meeting has gone as far as it can," Vivian said. "Now I'll talk with Mr. Walker and I'm sure . . ."

"In no other profession," Walker declared, "would one be subject to such slander and innuendo. We're treated no better than servants here. Teachers in Japan, even in Russia, are accorded respect automatically. The system is quite different in other countries."

"I see," Charlie said. "That's it, then. It's system, is it? That's what people like you love. I've sat here and listened to you. I'll bet I know what goes on in your class." Charlie's chin was trembling. "Rules. Regimen. It's system, all right. You need the system, don't you, because you can't earn your way without it. If the kids don't like you, if they fail because you're a lousy teacher, if you insult them because they don't understand or can't live up to your expectations, then it's the system you cry about. You wouldn't have to put up with this in Japan or Russia, would you? Well, this is America. Thank god, this is America. Here you have to earn respect."

Charlie looked at David. He couldn't tell if his son was proud or embarrassed, but it suddenly didn't matter. Right now he wouldn't go across the street for the boy.

Vivian came from behind the desk, but Charlie moved before she could step between them.

"That's the trouble," Charlie went on. "Mister, you don't know what system is. You ought to come out into the real world. Eight, ten, twelve and twenty minute tardies respectively. Shit, come out where the rules are measured by dollars, buddy. Hundreds of thousands, millions of dollars, and your ass on the line. Rules and systems, that's what's wrong, and small fry like you love it. Without your damned tenure, you'd be out managing a hamburger stand. Don't pull me." He tugged his arm from Marian's grasp. "Well, the system stinks," he finished, "and so do you."

Tiny flecks of foam had appeared at the corners of Walker's mouth. He held his briefcase across his chest like a catcher's vest.

"Let me out of here!" he shouted. "Let me out of here right this minute!"

108

The space between the desk and the row of chairs was no wider than a man with his legs apart, and Charlie stood there facing the teacher.

"It's no small wonder your son is having trouble," Walker smirked, "with such a role model."

Charlie made a move. It was like something out of a kung fu movie he had seen on television. Walker swung the briefcase. The force of it all carried Charlie over the desk and against the wall. Marian screamed and David said, "Holy shit."

Stuff came down from the wall. A motto encased in glass that read Help Me To Understand shattered across the desk. Diplomas fell. A plaque from Rotary International struck Charlie on the head and a philodendron toppled, spilling potting soil onto the dun colored carpet. Charlie hit the floor. He was exhiliarated. He hadn't been in a fight since Muzzy Meyer in the tenth grade. He tried to jump up, his hands doubled into fists.

"Charlie!" Vivian cried.

His name in her mouth for the first time made him stop. He stood there. He felt fat and awkward. Two buttons had popped from his shirt. Walker had slumped into a chair, terrified.

"All right," Charlie said. "All right, all right."

David started to laugh, so Charlie slapped him. Marian turned on her heel and strode out of the office.

* * *

At five Charlie left the house and got into the BMW. "Jesus H. Christ, what are you trying to prove?" he asked. "Just what in the hell are you trying to prove now?"

"I'm not trying to prove anything," he replied.

"You could get your ass in a sling for that little effort, you know."

"He had it coming."

"He didn't have it coming. He had you going."

"It's the principle of the thing, then, goddamnit."

"What're you all of a sudden, with this principle shit?"

"Maybe it's honor, then."

"Honor my ass. You're lucky if you don't get sued."

"So are they all, all honorable men."

"Jesus H. Christ."

When he got to the track, she was already out. He parked the BMW along the street and sat for a time watching her.

The sun was just beyond the hills and the sky was red. She went round and round, her arms bent at the elbow, her head up and proud. She knew someone was in the car looking at her, it wouldn't be the first time, but it didn't matter. She went round that damned track and the hell with who was watching.

She had magnificient legs. If it weren't for the breasts, he would have held out for the legs, but the breasts were fine, there they were under a grey sweatshirt and simply fine. Her skin was very black, blacker than it had at first seemed, maybe because now he could see so much more of it. But it was getting dark.

Two houses up the street a guy was washing his car, and the hose was running over the hood. He was watching Vivian go round and round on the oval track.

Charlie got out of the car. He walked over to the chain link fence. She made the turn and came toward him. She looked at him and went by. Charlie watched her go around. She was going at that even pace and she came round and went by again and he tried to smile, but she kept on running. When she came around again, he put his fingers through the fence and pressed his face against it. She jogged over.

"I'm sorry," he said.

She looked at him and shrugged her shoulders.

"I live with that family, and I couldn't give a goddamn

about that English teacher, but I'm sorry because you were there and about Ruth Danilow, too."

She took a step forward and was at the fence. He could smell her and it was a beautiful, sweet smell.

"You knew Ruth."

"No, I didn't know her."

"But how did you know?"

"I saw her shopping sometimes at the Petrini's in Pleasant Hill."

She nodded. "She liked that store. Said the food was cleaner."

"I recognized the picture in the paper."

"Oh."

"I saw her do it."

She looked at him.

"I was on the bridge and she was there behind the wheel sobbing and all the traffic slowed down so I stopped and then she got out of the car and went over to the side of the bridge and just jumped over."

Vivian put her hand to her mouth.

He tried to push his fingers through the wire mesh to touch her. "And I can't shake it from my mind. I haven't slept a whole night since it happened. I keep waking up and seeing her standing there and then going over. I don't know why it's bothering me so much."

She leaned her head against the fence, and he could put his fingertips against her face.

"I'm sorry," he said. "I'm so sorry."

She was crying softly and he did not say anything. He just kept his fingers through the wire fence against her face. It was almost dark now, and the man up the street was watering the hood of his car.

When she was done crying, she looked up.

"I want you to help me," Charlie said. "How can I get

started? Will you please help me get started?"

CHAPTER SIX

The thought of running amused Charlie. It was such a damned self-conscious thing, plodding along the sidewalk, jogging in place at stoplights, skirting around pedestrians. And not smiling. He couldn't get over how all these running types never smiled.

"It must be real work," Charlie said, turning the car out of the driveway the following morning.

In fact, he was convinced that Walnut Creek was the running capitol of the world. There was a place on Bonanza where he liked to eat breakfast on the weekend and read the Chronicle, and more often than not a whole club of them, men and women, would come in after a run. They shoved three of four tables together against a wall, sitting in their campy little shorts, designer sweatshirts tied round their necks, Vaurnets hitched back on their heads, hundred dollar sneakers on their thumby feet. They ate pitted prunes and drank grapefruit juice and decaffeinated coffee and laughed out loud. Their health was obscene. Whenever they came in, he threw his money onto the table and went over to Denny's.

You couldn't drive anywhere in town without seeing people running. They were fanatics. They even ran at night, flourescent tape stuck to their heels. They ran with stereos strapped to their brains. They carried sticks or wore weights around their wrists. They ran through the park in herds. They ran races up and down the San Francisco hills. They ran across the Golden Gate Bridge. They ran cross country. They ran by his house.

He would go to Harrah's to shoot crap, and they'd be slogging through the snow. Towels wrapped around their heads, like fighters, they splashed through the rain. At midnight, driving to the condo at Zephyr Cove, he'd see them running through the cold night air. There must be a regular organization of them all over Northern California, and they agreed to be out in public whenever he was.

"Crazy," Charlie said, heading for the high school parking lot. "I don't want to be seen on the fucking street with any of them."

To his thinking they were like those aerobic broads with their stupid chatter and bouncy can-can dances. "Or bird watchers. People who swim in the bay in December. What the hell is it around here?"

The high school lot was empty, except for a black Corvette, one of the older models with the rolled over front fenders and the hind quarters of a bullfrog. Vivian had struck him as the punctual sort and he was a good ten minutes late himself, so he was not sure where to wait, or maybe she had changed her mind and wasn't coming, but she hadn't struck him as that type either.

As the BMW moved into the lot, he was surprised to see the door of the Corvette open and two long, tapered, dark legs swing out. He pulled alongside and reached over for the handle.

"Hi," he said.

"Hello," she smiled, getting in.

"That machine is yours?"

114

"You don't think it fits the image of a high school counselor?'

"You have to admit it's a little racy."

"A holdover from the marriage. My husband called it a pussymobile. He was driving it when he met me. He got the furniture. I kept the pussy. And what about you?" She tapped the dashboard.

"Pride of ownership. Mechanical excellence not found in American automobiles. Rack and pinion steering. Independent suspension. Four wheel disc brakes."

"C'mon."

"Status symbol, then. I like driving it. So what?"

"Why not?"

"Why not. So where are we going? Keep in mind this whole thing embarrasses the hell out of me."

"Going off with a black woman?"

"No. I'm going to work. Didn't you know?"

"I see. That sets a terrible precedent. You work in the city, don't you?"

"Yes, I do that."

"Let's go over there. I know a nice little shop on Union."

"All right."

"This doesn't embarrass you, does it really?"

"No, it doesn't. Does it you?"

"Maybe it does both of us a little. Dishonesty is always embarrassing."

"No, it's not."

"Someplace inside it is. Haven't you learned that yet? So you told your wife."

"OK. So I'm going to the office. I disgust myself."

"No, you don't. You're proud of yourself. But you shouldn't be proud of yourself that way. Embarrassment would be better. It would at least be honest."

"Maybe I should go back to school."

115

"I'm black and the worst thing to be if you're black is dishonest. You can't lie to yourself, not for a minute, because all around you is lying, and if you lie to yourself, you're gone."

"Funny, I never felt that way about being honest."

"You wouldn't. You're white. You have plenty of lying room. If you're black, all you've got is yourself, and in there there's no room for lying."

She tapped her chest.

"Why are you doing this with me today, then?"

"I didn't like how your wife walked out on you."

"That's just her way. When she gets uncomfortable, she walks."

"That's no way."

"You felt sorry for me."

"Some."

"You didn't pity me."

"No."

"I like you."

"You like my body."

"No, seriously, I like you."

"You don't like somebody you don't know. You're attracted maybe. Maybe you've got the hots. But like is something for when you know somebody."

"You don't like me, then."

"I liked it when you took a swing at Walker. He's an arrogant sonofabitch."

"But you wouldn't let him know that."

"Not professional."

"Isn't that being dishonest?"

She looked at him. "Now I'm beginning to like you. With the people with whom I have to be professional, I'm aloof. I just don't talk with them apart from my duties, and I don't socialize with them outside of school. When you work with

116

people, you work with people. Know what I mean?"

"Tell me about it."

"And I like how you were about Ruth."

He saw it again. The wind blowing the skirt about her legs. The little hitch, as though she were trying to reach something from a top shelf. And then the roll. He remembered now that both her shoes had come off.

"I can't understand it," he said.

"She was so upset. Her husband . . ."

"No, I don't mean that."

She watched him.

"I mean me," Charlie said. "I can't understand it with me. What does it have to do with me?"

"You saw it."

"That's why you decided to do this, I suppose."

"That's perverted."

"So what?"

Her face lost all expression. "Maybe there's some truth in it, then. I don't know. You caught me by surprise last night. I cried. I was through with crying, but I cried. It was because you saw her. You were the last. Ruth was my good friend. She was naked white, but she stood next to me when a bunch of honky bastards wanted my scalp. Maybe it is perverted."

"Maybe you want me to leave now, then."

"Oh, cut it out."

"I was only trying to say that I can't understand what's going on inside."

"I'm saying I love my friend and you made a fool of yourself in my office and I liked it somehow, so maybe everything's connected. If I were God, I could explain it, but I'm not. I'm just going along and I don't know why. Now what are we waiting for?"

It was a little shop. Boxes lined the walls. There were kiosks filled with tennis shoes and sweat socks. There were posters of people running or peddling ten-speeds. There were biker helmets, tennis rackets, those campy shorts with slits down the sides and matching velour pants and tops with stripes along the arms and legs. A muscular little man with a beard and wearing a black and white referee's shirt, black cotton pants and sneakers came over to them smiling.

"May I help you folks?"

"I was thinking about maybe getting into jogging or something," Charlie said. "I need some stuff, I guess."

"I see," the man said. "You don't know at the moment if you're going to be serious about it."

"Well," Charlie said.

"He's serious," Vivian said.

"The most important thing is, of course, shoes," the man said. "Let's go outside for a moment."

Vivian smiled and Charlie shook his head.

"Now," the man said once they were on the sidewalk, "I want you to just run up the street twenty strides or so and then turn and run back."

"You want me to run out here?"

"Just make it an easy gait, Sir."

"Run, Charlie," Vivian grinned.

He shrugged and set off. He felt like a fool. The people in traffic watched. He felt the roll of his stomach lift and drop against his belt. "Jesus H. Christ."

"That's fine, fine," the salesman said when he returned. Charlie heard his heart beating. Vivian was laughing. He realized he had been showing off.

"What's it all about?" he asked.

"I need to watch the way you land on your feet. Also whether you carry your toes out or in. It helps us pick the right shoe for you. The right shoe is everything."

"Everything," Vivian said, winking.

They went back into the store. "Adidas makes a shoe that

I think will work," the salesman said. "Do you know your size?"

"Ten-D," said Charlie.

The salesman went in back and Vivian said, "You're on your way."

"To what?"

"To whatever."

"Running."

"You've been doing that for quite awhile, I suspect."

"Are you this tough on everybody?"

"Just on white-assed businessmen who want to get into my pants."

"And how many times has that happened?"

"Once or twice. I'm very choosy."

"All right, I don't want to get into your pants. Now lighten up."

"There you go being dishonest again. You're with me, you're going to have to be honest. What's wrong with my pants?"

"Nothing's wrong with your pants."

"Well, why don't you like them?"

"I never said I didn't like them."

"Well, say it then."

"For chrissake, I like them."

"No, I want to hear it."

"I like your goddamn pants."

"All of it."

"All of what?"

"Say all of it. C'mon."

"I want to get into your pants. All right."

"Didn't sound very convincing."

"I want to get into your goddamn pants."

"And do everything."

"What?"

"You know. You want to suck my nipples. You want me to
go down on you. You want to take me from the rear. You want
to do it on the floor. Or in the bathtub. Or on the sofa with the
TV on. Or right there in your own house when your sweet
wife is visiting her sister in Bakersfield."

"Her sister lives in Ukiah."

"Don't change the subject."

"Jesus H. Christ."

"You want it so much you'd consider marriage. We'd
break the color barrier and live together in Walnut Creek and
go to the Savoy together and Max's and we'd run down Main
Street together on a Sunday morning in matching outfits, you
can't help it, you're falling in love with me. It's the beginning
of a new world. I have a dream. I have a dream."

"Will you cut it out. How did you get into counseling
anyway? Go stand over there. Pick out some sweats or
something."

"I don't want to go over there."

"Will you please just go over there. The goddamn
salesman's coming back. Go on."

"I want to see how the shoes fit."

"Will you go over there for chrissake. I have a hard-on."

"See," she said, laughing. "You're getting the idea. That's
the most honest thing you've said so far."

She flipped through the velour pants and shirts while the
salesman removed his dress shoes and cinched up the
sneakers. "How do those feel?" the salesman asked.

Charlie stood up and walked around. He flexed his knees.
Vivian grinned and made her thumb and first finger into a
circle.

"Fine, I guess."

"They feel all right."

"They feel fine."

"You'd like to see some running suits now?"

120

"Why not?"

"This one," Vivian said, holding up a purple set with pink stripes.

"My god," Charlie said.

"This?"

"No, no."

"How about red?" she asked, putting it against his chest.

"I don't want red."

"Why not? You look good in red. You need something bright."

Charlie wiped his brow. "Just plain. A plain pair of sweats."

"White, then. To match your hide."

"C'mon."

"Black." She winked.

"For chrissake." But he was laughing.

"Grey?"

"That's it."

"Somewhere in between. Non-committal."

"I'm not trying to prove anything."

"A BMW and grey sweats. C'mon, Charlie."

"Just give me the grey. Size large."

"Large? They shrink."

"Extra-large."

"And a few pair of socks," Vivian said, turning to the salesman, who was manufacturing an appropriate expression.

"Then can we get out of here?" Charlie whispered.

"I know just the place," she said.

They drove to a secluded beach. He had never been there, though he had seen pictures of it on posters and even an item on the 6 o'clock news. The view of The Golden Gate was spectacular, the towers above a sheet of fog and the great platform standing upon the ice blue water that spread westward into the Pacific.

"I'm glad my office isn't here," Charlie said. "If I had that outside my window, I couldn't get anything done."

"It is lovely, isn't it?"

"And cold," Charlie said, rubbing his hands. "What the hell are we doing out here?"

"You want to start running, don't you?"

"Out here?"

"Beaches are fine places to run. Easy on the feet. Beautiful views. Seagulls shitting everywhere. You'll love it. And there's no one around."

"I don't want to run today."

"Why not?"

"I'll get sweaty and smelly. I don't want to get sweaty and smelly."

"You can shower at my place."

"You're kidding."

"Why not? Just strip there in the car. I promise not to look. Take a turn up and back. You bought this equipment, didn't you?"

"Vivian."

"C'mon, get with the program. I want to check your style. You know. I want to watch how you land on your feet and if your toes go out or in. Makes a difference, they say."

Charlie undressed in the back seat and pulled on the sweats. Then he laced up the tennis shoes. It was the first pair he had owned in twenty years.

"All right," he said, stepping out of the car. "But I look like an idiot."

"You look like a slightly overweight business executive who's gone soft on life."

"What is this, a counseling or a training session? If it weren't for my goddamn doctor, I wouldn't be out here, you know."

"Blood pressure?"

"A little."

"And weight?"

"Twenty pounds."

"Good. You'll be in shape in no time."

"For what?"

"To be hard, what else?"

She began walking across the beach to the place where the tide had made the sand damp and firm. He followed.

"This is best," she said. "Just go along there above the surf. The footing will be good. Don't hurry. A nice, easy pace. Don't lift your legs high and then plop down. Just slide your feet along. Keep your knees flexed. Don't land on your toes. You'll work that back tendon too much. Just slow and easy. Jog fifty and walk fifty. Like that. Go up to that mound on the right and turn and come back."

"This is silly."

"You don't believe that. Now go on."

He started off. He thought he should do the running first. He swung his arms across his chest. He rolled his shoulders. He stretched his legs. His head was up. His chest was out. His feet came down plop, plop. That's how he had seen them all do it on the streets. Plop, plop. Plop, plop.

"You're going too fast," Vivian called. "This isn't a race, white man. Slow it down."

He was thankful. After forty yards his heart was grinding. He had to open his mouth to breathe. A bit more and he heard Vivian yell, "Walk!"

He counted fifty slow paces. A damp breeze was blowing off the sea. It cooled his face. He liked the feel of the sweats in soft folds over his arms and legs and across his stomach. Then he ran and counted fifty and walked and he was at the mound.

He turned. Vivian waved. He started off but skipped the last walk and ran the hundred paces. He shouldn't have.

When he stopped before her, he had to bend over and grab his knees.

"You're not going to get into my pants if you're stupid," she said. "Showing off is for high school kids."

"Whew," he gasped.

"And you're going to have to give up the cigarettes."

"Shit," Charlie said. "You're as bad as the doctor."

"You asked for my help. When you catch your breath, go down the beach the same way. But take smaller strides. Stay within yourself. The secret is to find a relaxed stride, something you can live in yard by yard. This is for you, remember. It isn't for anybody else."

Charlie set off at an easy lope, which was just a bit more than a brisk walk.

"Good," Vivian called. "That's the way. Take it slow. Stay within yourself."

He moved on down the beach counting to fifty. Then he walked. It was a fine day, he decided. "It's a goddamn beautiful day."

He blew and inhaled, blew and inhaled.

"For me and nobody else."

He was walking. The sea gave off an effervescence. Tiny jewels of light gleamed above the blue swells. Combs of white rolled here and there. Far off, the line between ocean and sky was like something at the bottom of a canvas.

"Goddamn."

He set off. He pulled the steps in a bit more. That was it. That's it. That's the best yet. He felt the heels come down and the pads behind the toes and then the toes. That's it. Easy. Easy. He went on down the beach. Twenty-five. Twenty-six. He was starting to blow, but that was all right. It felt good to make his body work. "Just make it work." Thirty-seven. Thirty-eight. He was pushing against something but it was all right. Fifty.

He stopped and turned around. Vivian waved. He waved back. "Once more." He started walking. He went thirty paces before he saw the thing gleaming at the water's edge. The tide was apparently going out because one last heave had brought it in, and now the edges of foam only licked and curled it.

He did not move. The sea touched the thing. It rolled and fell back, rolled and fell back. Waving hello. Waving goodbye.

"My god," Charlie said.

There was some amount of time that passed but he could not tell. He heard his name being called. Still he remained, watching the thing wave hello, goodbye.

"Charlie."

The thing was talking. It was calling him.

"Charlie, what is it? Are you all right? What's the matter?"

Vivian came up beside him. The thing hadn't spoken. It didn't know his name.

"This," he said, pointing.

"What is it?"

"This. It's red."

"It's red, so what? Just something somebody threw away."

"Ruth was wearing a red suit that morning."

Vivian stared.

"It doesn't have any pockets or zippers or anything, does it?" he said.

"Charlie."

"Does it?"

"I don't know. What are you saying?"

"I'm not saying anything. I don't want to say anything." He picked up a piece of driftwood.

"What are you going to do?"

"You'll recognize it, won't you?"

"Don't touch it, Charlie."

"Don't you want to know?"

"I don't want you to touch it, you hear me?"

"Then I don't want to know either."

He sat down on the sand.

"What are you doing?"

"Just a minute," he said.

"Charlie."

"I want to sit for a minute."

He watched the final reach of the surf open the cloth ever so gently and then fall back, pulling it closed again. A thousand tiny bubbles exploded and the cloth shone with a hot red light.

"Isn't that a sleeve?" Charlie said. "Right there. That's a sleeve, I'll bet."

"Charlie, I want to go."

"A skirt wouldn't do like that. It's the jacket. I'm sure it's the jacket. But what's it doing here? Right here, right now?"

Vivian turned and moved off up the beach toward the car. "We're going."

"That current out of the bay is tricky," Charlie said. "When the tide's just right, people can get carried under the Gate. It happens. They find them out by the Farralones. It happens all right. There's something here. Jesus H. Christ, there's something definitely here."

He stood, the driftwood in his hand. Vivian ran at him and threw her arms around his chest. She was big and rawboned. Her weight took him to the sand. She tried to straddle him, slapping at him.

"Hey," he yelled.

"I said leave it alone, leave it alone, goddamn you. It's something somebody lost or somebody threw away. What difference does it make? Why don't you leave it alone the way I asked? Do you think I need anymore? Do you think I want anymore to be told she's dead forever? I've seen her beautiful, running naked in the wind, free as the sunlight, the two of us running. Do you think I need to look into a hollow coat and imagine her melting someplace out there under the fish and slime? Now take me home, take me home." She punched him weakly. "Sonofabitch, you made me do it all over again." And she put her head on his chest.

He held her and looked at the sky. There was sand in his hair. He could could feel it under the small of his back down in behind the sweats.

"All right. All right. I don't know what this is but I'm sorry. OK? I want you to tell me, that's all. I want to know what's going on. There's something happening here. You have to tell me or I'll go nuts. We'll go now, but I want to know why Ruth committed suicide."

"What do you expect me to say?" She held herself still.

"I don't even know what to ask. I feel this, whatever it is, closing in on me, and all I did was stick my fucking tongue out."

"What do you mean?"

"She went by me before the Caldecott. I was talking to myself, so what? So she was laughing. So I stuck my tongue out. The next time I saw her she was slumped over the steering wheel crying, and I watched her get out of the car and go over the edge. That's all, and every day I feel worse. So I have to know. What's going on?"

"All right." She sat up and studied him. "I'll answer your questions, if that will help."

They stood and she took his hand. They walked away up the beach. He paused a moment and looked back. The red cloth was perfectly still, shining in the grey light.

"Where does Abe Danilow work?"

"For an outfit called Eisner Corp."

* * *

He was quiet. It was odd to be driving the BMW in

127

running sweats and tennis shoes. It made him feel as though he didn't truly own the car. It was a kind of crazy little thought, but he found himself coming to it again and again all the way through town.

For an inevitableness had overtaken Charlie, and when his mind went down, it would flounder up and cling to this crazy little flotsam of thought. Here he was driving his $50,000 silver machine from the Bavarian woods in dirty sweats and tennis shoes, and there was sand on the glove leather seats and on the floormats, could you beat that? And he would cling there, rescuing himself from going down again.

He took the Embarcadero along the waterfront, and when he drew near the Ferry Building, he pointed at his office window.

"So that's where you run the world," Vivian said.

"Not quite," he replied.

"What do you do, then? Up there."

"I'm not really sure," he said.

"You're kidding."

"I could ask my secretary."

"You don't like it."

"Sometimes I don't." He looked at her. "Sometimes more than sometimes."

"Do you make something?"

"You mean me? The company makes things. Actually there are smaller companies making things. I administrate. I tell people what to do and they go tell other people and those people tell the people in the companies and they make things. I don't make anything specifically. Oh, wait a minute. I make money. That's what I make."

"You're cynical."

"What does Abe Danilow do?"

"He's a chemist."

"What does a chemist do?"

"I don't know. Make things, I suppose."

"He doesn't talk about it?"

"He's always working on some project or other. He never says much."

"Do you see him?"

"We had dinner. But when somebody dies, it's like a divorce."

When they got to the bridge, he wanted to show her the place where Ruth had jumped but thought better of it. Instead he said, "That was pretty ridiculous, on the beach, I mean. Wasn't it?"

"You mean me?"

"Oh, no, of course not." He patted her knee. It was the first time he had touched her. "I made you cry and that was ridiculous. Then the business about the red thing, that was ridiculous too. I don't want you to cry, but you can understand that about the red thing, can't you?"

"You've never seen anybody die before."

Charlie considered a moment and then said, "I saw my father die. It was after I was married and we were still living in the valley and the kids hadn't come along. One night I got a phone call and it was this woman my father had been screwing for twenty years and my mother knowing all the while. He was on the floor in the woman's house and she called me. Two firemen had an oxygen mask over his mouth and nose and a doctor was pounding his chest. His face was blue. His body flopped like a fish everytime the doctor hit him. But I didn't cry. I didn't even think about crying. I was just mad as hell, that's all. I haven't told anyone that story."

"Why did you tell me the story?"

"I don't know."

"You don't."

"Maybe I know. Sure. Some I know."

"You like me."

"Yes."

"I like you too. But that's not why."

"No."

"It was the beach."

"Yes."

"The cloth made you tell me."

"You believe that? I guess it did. But I wouldn't have told just anyone."

"No. But it's my relationship to it, that's what counts."

"The cloth."

"Ruth. Maybe it was her coat. I don't say it wasn't."

He looked at her. "That's a turn around."

"Maybe not. It's important to you that it could be Ruth's jacket and equally as important to me that I didn't want it to be. We both want the same thing. I loved Ruth. The question is, why do you want her?"

When they got to the parking lot, Charlie reached across and opened the door.

"Shower?" she asked. "Or do you intend to go home looking like that?"

Charlie laughed. "I didn't know if you were serious."

"Follow me."

She climbed into the Corvette, showing those shapely dark legs. He followed her to the section of town near the Bart station, where years ago walnut orchards had been uprooted to make way for office buildings and apartments. The offices had walls made of wrap around glass that shone like gun metal, and there were fountains that the kids periodically laced with soap. After awhile the old apartments were converted to condominiums. They sprouted here and there with names like Willow Run and Sunset Oaks. Redwood veneer. Planter boxes. Rolled lawns. And among them, like forgotten weeds, a few clapboard homes with brick walks and picket fences that had been built some time before the Second Great War. It was into the driveway of one of these that Vivian turned the Corvette.

He parked the BMW behind her and got out. When he looked over the waist high fence, he saw that a portion of lawn was dead in a rather odd pattern.

"Do you like that?" she asked.

"It's too bad. Some kind of disease?"

"You got that right. Come over here." He walked through a small gate and up onto the front step. "Now look."

The dead grass was in the shape of a rude cross.

"Nice, isn't it? I woke up one morning and there it was. Gasoline. They torched it. Smelled like burnt hair. Still want to come in?"

"What do you mean?"

"You hesitated when you got out of the car."

"I was thinking about carrying my clothes into the house. It felt funny."

"What with the neighbors and all."

"C'mon," he said. "I was thinking about you, too."

"The hell you say."

"Bright professional black woman having a white-assed honky get out of a fancy car and come into her house carrying his clothes. C'mon."

"If there's truth in that, then I appreciate it," she said.

He looked at the grass. "Who the hell would do such a thing?"

"There was an article about it in the paper."

"That was you, then. You mean they did this?"

"Welcome to my world."

"We don't have that shit out here."

"Honey, we have that shit everywhere."

She opened the door and went in. He stood there.

"It's all right if you want to go, Charles," she said. She

had moved to one side and he could not see her. "If you want to go, go on ahead. It wouldn't matter, really. Maybe it's asking a lot. You never know. Go on and go if you like. We could have dinner some time in the City. Call me at school."

"What are you talking about?"

"It would be asking a lot, wouldn't it? That's how it's going through your mind. What's in it besides a little black pussy. Pussy's pussy. And when a man's unhappy and not bad looking with plenty of money, what's to worry? And besides, they're probably watching from across the street anyway."

"What?" he said.

"Don't turn around. You'll just have to make up your mind, that's all. They have your license number by now, but for all they know it's just business. A white man and a nigger woman doing a little business. That is, if you just go to your car and drive away. Because if you get your clothes and come in, they'll think something else, and then they'll hate you for what they're thinking."

Charlie waited in his sweats and tennis shoes. A fiery buzz touched the back of his neck. He moved his hand to it. Then he stepped from the porch and went to the car. Across the street was a group of peach-colored condominiums and further on, an older white stucco home. He looked back. Vivian had not closed the door. He looked at the cross scorched into the lawn. Vivian kept the door open. He unlocked the trunk and removed his clothes.

When he got inside, she pushed the door shut with a foot and put her arms around him. "Thank you," she said. She kissed him.

"You mean those people live across the street from you?"

"No," she said. "They saw the article in the paper too. It made them nosier than when I first moved in."

"Where?" he asked.

"That front window on the stucco house. I'll go out and

132

check the mail."

She went to the box and returned.

"What did you see?"

"The curtains moved."

"There you are. Now they know you."

"They know me?"

"Of course not. They just know a white man came into the nigger's house and we're in here doing fellatio and cunnilingus."

"You're crazy."

"Prophetic."

"You don't seem scared."

"Of you?"

"Jesus, no. Of them."

"Not them."

"The ones who did the lawn."

"Yes. I'm scared of them."

It was a very pleasant room. There was something that had been in the oven and the smell was sweet. The house was small and everything was straight forward. A sofa. A few chairs. A little fireplace and next to that a portable TV.

"So I want to tell you something," he said.

"What is it?"

"I don't want you to use that word anymore."

"What word?"

"You know what word."

"Nigger."

"I don't like it when you say it."

"Haven't you ever called anyone nigger?"

"Sure."

"To their face?"

"No, of course not."

"People are niggers behind their backs to polite, courteous folks you have to do business with. Or as long as

133

the politeness lasts or they don't get angry at you. Then when you walk away, they say 'fuckin' nigger.' They turn to their other folks after you're gone and say 'fucking goddamn nigger.'"

"Don't say it."

"Those who did the lawn hate me. They say it."

"Do you know who they are?"

"No."

"Not anything about them?"

"Not anything but their hate. And they don't know me. They don't want to know me. They hate, that's what they know. It gives them power. They need their hate. It keeps them from being afraid."

"That's ugly," Charlie said.

"You don't have to say that."

"What do you mean I don't have to say it?"

"You don't have to prove anything."

"I'm not proving anything."

"Sure you are. You're tolerant."

"I'm not condescending."

"Who said you were? But tolerant isn't so hot."

"What am I supposed to say?"

"Say it once, then."

"I don't want to say it."

"Say it for all the time and all the shit."

"No."

"Say it for all the years when it didn't matter, when you just changed the channels or turned the page, when you looked at something else because you were embarrassed, or you were too embarrassed to be embarrassed. C'mon, say it."

"Nigger," Charlie said. He was shaking.

"Say it once more because you'll never leave your wife, you'll never marry me, you'll never be in love or live with me, you'll never even speak about me to someone to ease your soul when you doubt yourself. Say it because we'll be friends and that's more important than anything. Say it because it's the enemy of everything we'll ever be."

"I don't want to say it."

"Say it."

"Nigger," he whispered.

"You won't say it again."

"No, I won't."

"Not even if someone really is a nigger."

"I won't."

"Thank you, Charles," she said, kissing him. "Now I'll get you a fresh towel."

CHAPTER SEVEN

Charlie stood at the window looking out at the bay. There were no ships this morning. Not even a sailboat. It wasn't hard to imagine a time when there were no people. Only grizzly bear. Deer grazing down to the water's edge. Wildcats. The rivers swarming with fish. The fog rolling through the delta. The wetlands covered with geese. Lightning storms above the Sierra. And silence. Silence in the reeds and along the gullies. Silence like a hill shutting out the sea.

There was a tapping at the door and Charlie said, "Come in."

"What is it, old man?" Frank asked, holding onto the knob.

Charlie did not turn around. "Come on over here," he said.

Frank closed the door and walked to the window.

"It's still not as good as my view. You ought to see my view at sunset these days. The Golden Gate really catches fire."

"The Safecon Project," Charlie said.

"The what?"

"Safecon. Ever hear of it?"

"I never heard of it. What is it?"

"Look at that folder on my desk."

Frank picked up the manila folder. "What are you doing with an Eisner file?"

"Janet got it for me. But never mind that. Open it."

"All right. I'm opening. But it makes me a little nervous, I want you to know. The merger hasn't been finalized, Charlie. Strictly speaking, this isn't yet our business. Who's Abraham Danilow?"

"A chemist. Read that list of work he's into."

"All right," Frank said, running down the page. "So Item 5 is the Safecon Project. It's an Eisner Corp job. So what's the point?"

"When I was working with the old man to set this deal up, I studied all the divisions of Eisner Corp. I looked at all the work the company's involved in. I never once heard of anything called Safecon. I never came across the word in any document. And I studied the infrastructure and business affairs of the entire company. I had to, didn't I? But there it is. Safecon. What is it?"

"Charlie," Frank said, "maybe it's just a discontinued project, an experiment that didn't pan out. They just haven't taken it off the books yet."

"It's not in the books. I've seen the books and it's not there. But it's in that file. Danilow's file."

"Maybe the file's old."

"Look at the date on the inside cover."

"Two months ago."

"Two months. And I've been working on this deal for the last six months."

"OK."

"OK. So either somebody's covering something or somebody's working on a project they don't want us to know about. Either way, something's going on. And there shouldn't be anything going on, right, Frank? The two companies are merging. We're supposed to know everything about everything. So what's the Safecon Project?"

"I don't know."

"Maybe we're not supposed to know."

"What are you saying?"

"You tell me."

"You're nuts."

"Sure I am."

"You snorting shit again?"

"I gave it up."

"You're nuts. What you're saying here is nuts, you know that."

"What was I saying?"

"You're not supposed to be poking around, Charlie. Where'd you get that file?"

"What do you mean I'm not supposed to be poking around?"

"I mean it's none of our business yet. You might be doing something illegal. That's all."

"It is our business. The papers are on Carpenter's desk. You talked to Carpenter lately?"

Frank took a step away and looked out the window.

"We haven't had a meeting since that big blowout with old man Eisner."

"You've seen him."

"I see him as a matter of business."

"What business ?"

"Say, what is this?"

"I don't know. What is it, Frank?"

"Am I being faulted here because I'm concerned? The company is all I care about. It's all I truly care about."

"Of course. Ever since the split from Julie. By the way, do you ever see Julie?"

Frank's face went white. "Of course. Once in a while. You

can't help that."

"I've never seen her since I stopped seeing her. Funny."

"What kind of crack is that?"

"It isn't a crack. Just an observation. You work in a big city, you wonder if you'll ever see somebody, and you don't."

"Have you wanted to see her?"

"No. I thought I saw her once in Ghiradelli Square a couple of years back leaning over a rail looking at Alcatraz. But I didn't go over."

"That's the difference between you and me. I would have wanted to know."

"What?"

"If it was Julie."

"Why don't you want to know what Safecon is?"

Frank stood still and looked at the bridge.

"It's none of my business."

"The company is your business. Truly. Remember?"

Frank turned. "Don't pull that crap, Charlie."

"You ought to be proud of me. You've always bitched about my attitude."

"Your attitude hasn't changed that I can see. I don't know what you're trying to get at, but it's not the company you're concerned about."

"If I'm truly concerned about the company, I'll leave well enough alone, right? That's what you and Carpenter talked about. Leaving well enough alone."

"You shouldn't be poking around those files. I know that."

"Is that what you talked about?"

"No."

"Did he mention Danilow?"

"The first time I saw the name was today on that folder. I wish I hadn't looked. Whatever it is you're involved in, now you've involved me."

140

"You talked about being involved then."

Frank didn't say anything for a time. He put his hands in his pockets. "I met Carpenter one afternoon. He was going down to maintenance to tinker with a copier. I told him I wanted the job, that's all. I could do one hell of a job as president. You know I could. There's nothing wrong with my wanting to be president."

"Nothing," Charlie said.

"Every fellow has to look to his own interests. He has to watch out for himself."

"I agree."

"You don't have a lock on it just because you helped set it up."

"That's just my job."

"We're all qualified. Every one of us."

"Is that what he said?"

"Everyone."

"That includes you then."

Charlie looked at the water beneath the bridge.

"Are you going to help me, Frank?"

"Help you what?"

Charlie grinned. "Move this desk. I want to bring it over here by the window. I want to be able to look out while I'm working. I don't know why I've had it turned around all these years. Take that end, will you?"

*　*　*

Charlie was sitting quietly watching the bay when the phone rang.

"It's the high school," Janet said.

"Jesus, what now?" After a moment he said, "Hello."

"Hello, Mr. Bredesen. This is Barbara Carruthers, the dean's secretary. We have your daughter Kelly here on school suspension. Could you come get her please."

"Suspension. What did she do?"

"She was distributing leaflets on the grounds this morning before class. When she was asked to stop, she wouldn't. She was suspended."

"For passing out goddamn leaflets?"

"I'm sorry, Mr. Bredesen. It's school policy."

"Where is Kelly?"

"She's sitting here in my office."

"Let me talk to her."

"Would you just please come get her, Mr. Bredesen. Someone will talk to you then."

"I just can't come and get her. Why didn't you call Mrs. Bredesen?"

"We tried to reach her at work, Mr. Bredesen. She's not there."

"What do you mean not there? Did you try my home?"

"Yessir."

In the long moment of silence Charlie tried to recall something but failed.

"I'd like to talk to Vivian Chalmers."

"That's not Kelly's counselor."

"That's my son's counselor. Would you put me through?"

When he heard her voice, Charlie felt relieved.

"And I thought you wanted to talk to me," Vivian said.

"I do. You don't know how much I do. But what's the crap with my daughter?"

"Was she one of the students involved in the demonstration this morning?"

"Demonstration? What was she doing, lying down in front of traffic?"

"I only heard about it. She must have been passing out brochures."

"Brochures. What brochures?"

"I have one right here in front of me. Anti-abortion."

"Jesus H. Christ."

142

"He would have approved."

"Cut it out. How serious is it?"

"A tempest in a teapot. We have to have our rules, you know."

"Would you take her in tow, Viv? They don't seem to be able to raise my wife, and I can't drive over there just now."

"I'll put her in the waiting room outside my office. It's comfortable and she can study. We'll call your wife on the half hour. Maybe we can scare her up and save you the trip."

"You're a princess."

"Black women aren't princesses. Are you running?"

"All the time."

"I mean really."

"I ran last night. I'm going again tonight."

"Why at night?"

"That's none of the neighborhood's business."

"Mr. Bredesen, I do believe you're embarrassed."

"I'm not embarrassed. Well, some, maybe."

"Good. That's a good sign."

"Will you stop counseling me."

"Somebody has to."

"And you're elected, I suppose."

"If I'm given a chance."

Charlie was looking at the bay and smiling. He had been smiling for the past two minutes. "Have dinner with me tomorrow night."

"How?"

"Take BART over after work. I'll pick you up at the Market Street Station. Around five?"

"Whatever train gets there at five or immediately thereafter."

"How will I recognize you?"

"I'll be wearing black."

"A lot of women wear black."

143

"You can't miss me. I stand out in a crowd. Even a crowd of black."

"You must be something special."

"I am."

"Even if you aren't a princess. How come you aren't a princess?"

"Black women don't have that kind of fantasy."

"How come?"

"Too much reality."

"That's a shame."

"Maybe not. Maybe we can have a little, if you want. It might be fun, who knows? I'll surprise you at the station. Look for a little fantasy surprise from a woman in black."

"You're crazy."

"So are you."

"I sure as hell like you."

"Jesus H. Christ, that's a 10-4, good buddy."

He put the phone down and stood at the window. He watched the water for a long time. He couldn't stop watching.

When he got home, Kelly was in her room, David was off at Missy Franklin's, the new girlfriend, and Marian was fiddling with the VCR in the family room. She had a drink in the other hand.

"Well, what's the verdict?" Charlie said.

"Seems our little girl has become an activist. Take a look there on the table. You want a drink?"

"Why not?"

Charlie picked up a black and white pamphlet with a drawing of a fetus curled up in a womb. A hand was in the womb with a pair of scissors. Charlie shook his head. Inside the pamphlet were pictures of other fetuses, some in garbage cans, some in cardboard boxes. Beneath the pictures were quotes from the Bible, examples from Nazi Germany, exhortations about sin and goodness, explanations of

144

abortion technology and promises of Jesus' love. Somehow the information about saline injection and vacuum aspiration did not bother Charlie. It was the hook into religion that bothered him. He recognized the name of Kelly's church on the back page.

"She has to stay home for three days and then make up the work she's missed when she goes back," Marian said.

"I see," Charlie said.

"Well, you don't seem very disturbed. I thought you'd hit the roof."

"I did, too."

"What is it?"

He shrugged. "I can't say."

She brought him the gin and tonic. He took a deep swallow and then another. She watched him.

"I'm sorry I wasn't there to pick her up right away. Kelly tells me you talked to Dave's counselor, that Mrs. Chalmers. You could hardly keep your eyes off her the other day."

"What's that supposed to mean? She's the only one I knew to talk to. And since you weren't around. Where the hell were you anyway?"

"I went by the hospital to see Mother, of course. Things were slow at work. I just never know from one moment to the next. So I want her to know I'm there. I ran a few errands. Kelly only had to wait an hour."

"An hour's not bad."

"No, I didn't think so either."

Charlie sat on the sofa and spread his legs. "Are we on for dinner?"

"I can fix something for the two of us. David and Missy will be back later. Kelly's afraid to come down. You'd better go up and talk to her. She thinks you're going to bite her head off."

"All right," he said.

She took his glass and made him another drink. He held it for a moment and then set it on the table.

"Does it bother you if I look at other women?" he asked.

"I always supposed you did."

"But does it bother you?"

"Not particularly."

"What does that mean?"

"That's all. Except I guess it's natural."

"Is it natural for you?"

"To look at other men?"

"C'mon."

"Well, I suppose so. I usually admire bits and pieces, though. Traits or parts, you know what I mean. That's all you ever meet anyway, isn't it? Just parts? You would have to get to know somebody for anything else. And that always takes time. And nobody has any time anymore. I don't. Do you?"

"I don't have any time," he said.

"She does have big tits, though."

"Yours aren't so bad."

"Tits are tits."

"That's what I always say. Are you aware of how we go about doing this these days?"

"Doing what?"

"Checking out whether or not we're going to fuck."

"Is that what we're doing?"

"One of us just doesn't come out and say I want to fuck. We feint and jab. It kind of happens at the end, if nobody's knocked out."

"Have you ever had a nigger?"

"No. That's hitting below the belt, Marian."

"Down for the count?"

"No. Just cut that out. See?"

"I never had any desire for a black man. Or any other color. White's just fine with me."

146

"My white."

"Just fine."

"Does that mean you're committing yourself?"

"To what?"

"To fucking me tonight."

"I don't like that word."

"I don't like nigger."

He sat looking at her standing by the liquor cabinet. He thought he hated her but wasn't sure. He had lived with her most of his adult life. Maybe that's all it was. But hating her a little increased the desire.

"Don't you want your drink?" she asked.

"One's plenty. I'm running again tonight."

"Running. Following doctor's orders."

"Trying to."

"Do you like it?"

"It's too early to tell. I think so."

"How does it feel?"

"I get winded easily. Damned cigarettes. I've quit."

"My, you are taking all this seriously."

"Have to. Remember you want me to live."

"Love that income."

"That's it, all right."

"Of course not. Don't be cruel. Where did you get your running stuff, by the way?"

"Just sweats and tennis shoes. Picked them up in the city one day after work." When he lied, it made him want her even more.

"You smell after you run."

"I'll take a shower."

"No. I like it. I like the smell."

"Remind you of the good old days?"

"I even like your sweats. I like smelling them the next day."

He laughed.

"That's not sick," she said. "There's something about it. It makes me horny or something."

"I won't wash them until next week."

"I like it in the summer when the windows are closed and you get all sweaty on top of me. Did I ever tell you that?"

"No."

"I like it when you sweat."

"I love my work."

"I'll be all clean and fresh out of the shower, and you just come in from your run and do me."

"You like that. Do me. You like that."

"Just fuck me."

"I'll fuck you all right."

"Is it stiff?"

"Naturally."

"Show me."

He stood and lowered his trousers.

"You like that talk," he said.

"So do you. You used to like nigger."

He waited, feet apart, his dick sticking out above his shorts, and tried to remember when one of them had said I love you. He could not remember if he had even said it on his wedding day.

"I'll go on up and talk to Kelly," he said, zipping his pants.

"Take it easy."

"I have every intention."

He climbed the stairs and knocked on her door.

"Come in," the voice said.

Kelly was lying face down across the bed reading a magazine. She'd much rather be reading the Bible or some religious tract, he supposed, but the look in her eyes told him she was going to be defensive anyway.

"Well, we had an adventure today," he said.

"It wasn't my fault, Daddy, and it wasn't wrong."

"I didn't say it was wrong, Kitten."

"But you don't approve of it. You don't like it."

In the soft light of the bedroom her golden hair reminded him of another time, when she had been the final child and he had known that Marian had not wanted to be pregnant. She was somehow special to him then, like a foundling. They were both foundlings, and when he played "dirty water" with her on the floor, rolling her from one side of his body to the other, and she, giggling and squeeling when he threatened to tumble her from the clean into the dirty, begged him to let her be clean, just for always, please, Daddy, let me be in the clean water, and he held her in the air, lying on his back with the power to cleanse her or submerge her in filth, and now here she was, finding a muck of her own and dreaming that she was swimming in the milk of the Holy Virgin.

"The school does have rules," he said, "and I guess you broke them."

"Well, they're bad rules, then. We weren't doing anything wrong. We only want to save lives, that's all. We didn't hurt anyone."

"Nobody's questioning your motives, Kitten, just the methods. Rules are rules. There's a reason for them. That's a public school. People just can't use a public school to grind a personal axe."

"What does that mean?"

"You can't do your own thing just because you feel like it."

"Oh, what difference does it make?" she said, with one of those grimaces of closure with which the young try to end conversation with the old. "You don't care anyway."

"I care what happens to you."

"Sure."

"C'mon."

"You do?"

"You bet."

"You scare me sometimes."

"I scare myself."

"What does that mean?"

"I don't know."

"Why do you say things?"

"What things?"

"You know. Things that make me think I don't know you."

"Do I say things like that?"

"Lately you do. Sometimes."

"C'mon."

"I wish you cared about God."

"Kitten."

"It's important, Dad. It's the most important thing of all."

"I suppose it is."

"You see. You don't care."

"You don't know that."

"You don't act like you do."

"To you, maybe. That's because you have your mind made up that people only care if they hold hands around flagpoles or pass out pamphlets against school rules."

"You spend all your time making money. You don't understand."

"Hey, you're coming down pretty hard here. It's all that money that gives you this lovely life to which you've become accustomed, thank you."

"I don't need any of that."

"Ah, youth."

"I don't."

"Try living without it."

"I could. Jesus didn't need any of these things."

"Jesus lived 2,000 years ago. If he lived today, he'd need these things."

"No, he wouldn't. He'd help the poor and stuff."

"Would he bomb abortion clinics?"

"He might."

"He preached non-violence."

"So?"

"So think a little. Use your brain a little. That's what school is for. It's not for proselytizing religion."

Her face screwed up at the word. He could beat her at language but not at feeling. He admired her devotion, but it frightened him. Skepticism had always seemed more workable. You didn't belong to anything, but you could see things clearly enough. And with all the shit, that was all you could expect of anyone.

He wasn't sure that she was going to cry, but her eyes were wet.

"I don't want to fight, Kitten. What's done is done. I'm just concerned about you, that's all. I don't want you up here alone thinking I'm mad at you or thinking you're stupid or something. C'mon, take it easy. I'm just your old man. Old Mr. Dirty Water."

"Daddy."

"Remember?"

"Don't do that."

He raised his arms. "Look out. Here it comes. Here it comes. Down. Down. Look out."

"Stop it, Daddy. Please."

"It's OK."

"I don't want you to do that."

"But it's OK, Kitten. You're my girl."

"I'm your daughter."

"Hey, now."

"I'm just your daughter, Dad."

"C'mon. What is this?"

"I don't like that stuff anymore. You just do that to change me around. It isn't fair."

"I wasn't doing that."

"Just please."

"You missed the whole point, Kel."

"You always do that. And then you get mad."

"I'm not mad."

"If I care about things now that you don't care about, then that's OK, isn't it?"

"Did I say it wasn't?"

"I don't like being accused about the things I care about."

"You can care about anything you want. I don't care."

They sat on the bed. He looked at the wall. There was a cabinet he had found at a rummage sale when she was two. It had a glass door. He had stripped the cabinet and stained it. On the shelves were the dolls she had collected through childhood. There must be seventy-five of them, all cloth and rag and doughy porcelain. They were in rows, leaning against each other, dust lining the creases and folds. All the dolls of her childhood. She had kept the dolls anyway.

"This discussion isn't logical, you know that," he said.

"What do you mean?"

"A minute ago you were on me for not caring what you cared about. Now you're arguing that I should let you care about it and leave you alone. You don't care about what I care about."

"You care about making money."

He looked at the dolls.

"I told you I care about you."

She didn't say anything.

"Maybe it's OK to care about making money. You don't care about it because you don't have to worry about it. In this world today if you don't care about taking care of yourself, who's going to take care of you? And it takes money to do that. Don't you have some idea of what it's like outside the walls of this house? Don't you study that at school? Don't you and your friends talk about it? Look at your brother. He's a basket case. Playing the guitar and fantasizing about being a rock star. Failing classes. And all because he's afraid to graduate. Afraid to make the step because way down inside he knows. Maybe you're not old enough yet, but your brother knows. At least I think he knows. When he walks out there, the world will kick his ass because it doesn't care, Kel. It doesn't care about you and it doesn't care about me or your mother or Maju. If you haven't got the money to take care of you, then all that stuff you care about turns right around and walks away. You can pass out your pamphlets and have your prayer meetings because you can come home here at night and be safe and not worry. You have the luxury of caring about fetuses in garbage cans because I care about making money. And there are other things, see? I don't talk about them. I don't go around beating my chest about them, but I care. Why should I have to justify myself to a fourteen year old? I'm your father, goddamnit. Doesn't that count for anything?"

Kelly's face was pale. She sat on the edge of the bed. Her mouth was open and the air had dried her teeth. They looked like rabbit teeth. Little rabbit teeth, Charlie thought. Grind on me, you little rabbit teeth. Grind, you little bastards.

It hadn't gone right. He knew that it wouldn't when he walked up the stairs. He knew he should be a tolerant, loving, accepting father, but what was wrong with being tolerated, loved and accepted? He hated this whole thing of adolescence. He knew that someplace down the line, maybe as far down as the point when his hair was gone through the middle and his backswing was no better than an excuse for chopping weeds, his daughter would sit across from him in a home she had purchased (most probably with his help) and try to get him to be Mr. Dirty Water for his grandchildren. It made him angry to endure something ridiculous in the belief that he might be loved later.

"Hey, c'mon," he said, "this isn't good for either of us. Aren't you hungry?"

"No."

"Sure you are. C'mon down."

"I'll get something later."

"I'd consider it an honor and a privilege if you'd come on down and have a bologna sandwich with me. I'm buying."

"I'm just not hungry."

"You're just going to hold out, are you, Kitten? Don't be like your mother. Shouldn't some of that religion begin here at home? A little kindness right here at home?"

She stared at the wall and now the tears did come.

"I'm sorry," he said, putting his arm around her.

She nodded.

"That's good enough for me," he said, shaking her gently."That ol' nod. That baby's worth everything."

"Oh, Daddy," she said

"There's my girl." He hugged her. "How did it go at school? Were they rough on you?"

"No. Some of the kids were stupid, though."

"They said some not-so-nice things?"

"They're stupid. They don't know anything. But I liked Mrs. Chalmers."

"You did?"

"She was really nice. She let me in her office and we talked a little."

"Did you now?"

"She's black, you know."

"I know."

"I know you do." She looked at him.

"It might surprise you to discover that that is one of the things I'm caring about, Kelly. What did you discuss?"

"She said she had a friend who was very concerned about abortion too. There's a picture by her desk. She worked in a clinic or something."

"An abortion clinic."

"No, no, Dad. One of those places that helps people who get pregnant. Her husband was the one who was working on abortion."

Charlie took her arm.

"What did you say?"

"About what?"

"What you said, about this husband."

"The woman's husband worked in a laboratory or something."

"You said abortion. He was working on abortion."

"I don't know."

"Did Mrs. Chalmers say he was?"

"No."

"Well, why did you say it?"

"I don't know. She just told me her friend was upset at what he was doing, that's all. It had something to do with babies."

"With babies."

"We were talking about babies."

* * *

Charlie Bredesen had no friends. No real friends. Fred Bigelow lent him money. Ed Barton, Tom Oliva and Ernie Van Horton made up an adequate foursome. He enjoyed talking politics sometimes with Russ Harris, until Russ drank too much and started blubbering about marriage and alimony. Friends were like books. You kept them on the shelf and took them down when you needed to look up something.

So he didn't think of asking anyone to run with him, though he felt lonely and conspicuous at first out there on the street. Wasn't it stupid to choose to be alone when being alone was what he experienced so much of the time? What's more, in his mind he found himself associated with all those kooks, yuppies, freaks, jocks and nerds who filled the sidewalks every morning and afternoon. Either way he was in for it.

So he ran at night.

"All right," he said. "Left right, left right. Keep the knees bent. Nice and even. Jog fifty. Walk fifty. That's what the lady said. Heels first. Heels first."

He went around the block.

He didn't know what to do; that is, apart from the running. It seemed a rather useless time for the brain. The brain went bumping along. In fact, there was a job of convincing that had to be done. The brain would rather be on its ass watching television or with its face down between someone's legs or with its eye on a white, dimpled ball, fading just so over that treacherous pond and onto the fifteenth green. But here the brain was useless. It was along for the ride.

"Short steps," he said. "Remember, this is for you. This isn't for anybody else. Don't pump the legs. Easy. Easy. Just slide the feet. No plop plop. Jesus, no plop plop."

Three-quarters of the way around the block Charlie found the rhythm between the fifty steps walking and the fifty steps running. He knew it would be a simple matter when his wind came in to do it all running. "Just a little shorter on the step." Then he had it. Bouncing along, almost not an effort at all, just an easy, slow going along. In time, maybe just a little time, he would take it around the whole block and then another block. But the legs had to come in and the wind. They would come. And then it would be just an easy glide, step step, knees flexed, feet low, going on, on. It was like grooving a golf swing. After awhile it became mechanical, it happened. You swung, and the ball snapped down the fairway. That's how Nicklaus did it. And Palmer. Just snap, down the fairway, one more time like all those times on the practice tee. You don't even have to think about it.

He could see why so many of those jerks wore headphones when they ran. How awful to be imprisoned within a machine that merely plodded along. How boring to have nothing to do, and all the while you were doing so much, block after block you were running your heart out and here was your brain taking a vacation. It didn't seem fair, to Charlie's way of thought. Because in golf that's just when your brain had to work the most. Concentration, that was everything. It was how a pro made a hard shot look easy. He had tried to explain it to Eisner once at Cypress Point, but the old man had only grinned and patted him on the back.

"You ought to go on the tour," Eisner had said. "With a swing like that, you'd be a fucking good pro."

"I'm a good fucking pro already," Charlie had replied, sending the old man into a paroxym of laughter, who, when he thought Charlie wasn't looking, proceeded to kick his ball out from behind a pine tree.

"Babies," Charlie said.

When he made the turn back toward the house, he looked at his watch. It had taken him just under seven minutes. At that rate five or six times around would give him the half hour the doctor had prescribed.

The lights were on in the house. He loped by. It was an expensive house. All the houses in the area were expensive. BMW's were in the driveways. Mercedes. Volvos. Oriental gardeners came on Thursday (or was it Monday or Wednesday? There was always a pickup on the street hitched to a slatted trailer filled with the handles of lawnmowers, edgers and weedeaters). All year it seemed, while the patrons were away making money or preparing themselves for making it, Briggs and Stratton sheared the neighborhood, and the metallic whine of the two-cycle blower, perching now over here, now over there, was as commonplace and innocuous as the buzz of a fly. The only thing Charlie could not get used to was how the sprinklers came awake just before dawn, sprayed away for twenty minutes or so in some cautious sequence and then went quietly back to sleep. In the years that he had lived there he had never turned on an outside faucet or lifted a hose. He stepped out the door, holding his briefcase or his coat, and everywhere, about the lawn and shrubs, would be this silvery glistening, as though, in the night, a light rain had fallen. But only the edges of the driveway would be damp or a border of the sidewalk, maybe a half circle against the house. Everything else was dry, the street, the driveway, the roof, the car. Up and down the block it was the same. If the rain had come, it was a magical rain, appearing only above things that were green.

As he ran, the same invisible dogs barked. The same porch lights came on. Sometimes a curtain drew back and he saw a blank, white face peer out. In all the houses was the odd lavender glow of the television.

Charlie could feel his heart beating. "And that's all right," he gasped. "That's what it's supposed to do. Get the beats up and then rest. Whew. Make it work and rest. Sit on my ass too much. Got to pump the blood. Jesus H. Christ."

"Who's there?" he heard a voice call from beside a burgundy colored Saab.

"It's me. Charles Bredesen? I live around the block."

"What are you doing?"

"I'm running."

"What for?"

"I'm Charlie Bredesen," he said. "From around the corner?"

The man stepped out onto the sidewalk. He seemed a bit familiar, someone you see sometimes making a turn at an intersection or coming down an off ramp, and Charlie watched as the man tried to recognize him and then, perhaps, succeeded.

"Bredesen, huh? Hennesey here. Jim Hennesey. Heard the dogs barking again. You never know with the dogs barking."

"I guess not," Charlie said. "Sorry."

"Heart?"

"Exercise."

"Cholesterol," Hennesey said.

"What was it?" Charlie puffed. He could feel himself slowing down and he did not want to lose the sweat.

"Cholesterol. Too much. Eat fish. Eat chicken. My doctor wants me to eat broccoli. I hate broccoli. Can't be too careful around here, though. I heard the dogs barking again."

The man had grey hair.

"Sorry. I just live around the corner."

"I heard the dogs. It's those people of the darker persuasion. You understand." He patted Charlie's arm. "I heard the dogs. Haven't you seen them go by?"

"No," Charlie said.

"The dogs let you know. They don't like strangers. Particularly that kind. I know a few that are all right, but they don't go by late at night making the dogs bark."

"Who?" Charlie said.

"Who do you think? They're up to the rafters in Oakland. They're spilling over from Concord. You know."

Charlie ran in place.

"Well," he said.

"Heart?" the man asked.

"Blood pressure."

"Same thing. Eat fish. Eat chicken. Eat broccoli."

"I'm going around again now," Charlie said.

"The dogs will bark."

159

"I'll run on the other side."

"They've got dogs over there."

"I'll walk by here." He moved away.

"The dogs will bark," the man said.

Charlie shrugged, breaking into a run. He turned and waved. "Nice meeting you."

"Why don't you run in the park with the rest of the nuts?" the man called. "The dogs bark here."

By the time he had made the third loop, it was nearly ten o'clock. There was sweat on his forehead. There was sweat under his arms and down his back. There was something tightening in his legs. The bottoms of his feet throbbed.

Charlie felt good. It hurt, but that felt good, too. Sometimes the lights of a car came upon him. He turned his head and shut his eyes. He liked it in the dark with only the street lamps burning. It felt good to be running alone at night.

He made the fourth turn. The man with grey hair was standing on his front step, hands on his hips.

"So what?" Charlie said, wiping the sweat away.

As he approached the house, he saw that David's car was in the driveway to the far right in the shadow of the Cypress tree.

"What's he got the goddamned thing there for? He never parks it there."

It was time for the fifty paces walking and Charlie slowed. His shirt was stuck to his back. The folds of his shorts gathered into his ass. "I won't wear the damned things then," he said, wondering if he should buy a jockstrap to protect himself. "Hell, the Greeks used to wrestle naked."

Charlie looked at the car in the driveway. It was a Camaro, one of those eight cylinder '70s machines so enamored of by high school males. He had wanted to buy David something sensible when he had finished the drivers training course, a Beetle or a Dodge Colt, something with mileage and low maintenance. He had made a mistake buying the kid any machine at all. His father had not bought him a car until he had found a job after school and could make the payments. That was the way you learned responsibility. And you had to learn responsibility to grow up.

Whereas with Kelly he could not help feeling a profound difference, with David it was hard not to believe that, as a father, he had failed. There was something in Kelly he did not understand, a person inside he could not touch. In certain ways, certain intuitive ways, she was already smarter than he could ever hope to be. It had nothing to do with religion or that shit about abortion. No, Kelly Bredesen was a stranger, and the authority of being a parent was the only reason, he felt, that she allowed him sometimes to sit on her bed.

But with David everything was predictable. Even failure was no surprise. That had to do with boys these days, maybe, but maybe not. In harsher, more censorious moments, he believed that his son was as hollow as a basketball.

As Charlie drew near the driveway, he saw a head raise up in the back seat of David's car. The head went down immediately.

Charlie stopped. In a moment in which he understood completely and yet was confused, he turned to walk away and then hesitated.

"The sonofabitch."

Charlie stood on the sidewalk in the dark and watched the car. He tiptoed forward, then bent and shuffled like a crab. He got under the window on the passenger's side and listened. He heard a muffled sound, as though something had been kicked inside a closet. Then Missy giggled.

Charlie rose up slowly. He put his nose above the window sill. Then a bit more. He peered inside.

David had his pants down one leg, but the other, the one

161

on the seat, was still clothed, and the shoe was on. The girl had tried to position herself to receive all this love, but her legs hung open and stiff. They reminded Charlie of a naked mannequin in a department store window.

David's white ass bobbed and bobbed, and from time to time he glanced over the window up the street. The girl's legs were unmoving. Nobody said anything. It was work. David was driving a nail into a board.

Charlie watched. He could not see the girl's face. There was a clutter of material, an arm. A hand was on David's shoulder. David went up and down. The girl's legs hung clumsily, things thrown into a corner.

"He's doing it," Charlie whispered. "My son is fucking somebody. He's got a dick and he's doing somebody."

Then Charlie was lonely. He had never been so lonely. There had been plenty of loneliness before, but this was not the same. This was being different from something you had always belonged to and then realizing that all the while you had belonged to it, it had been exactly like you.

Charlie stared through the murky glass. There was no dramatic thread along which his life had run. He had not gone to war. In college there had been no team and something happening in the last of the ninth or on the two yard line. There had been no great struggle, no momentous development out of which decision or character is born. There had been no obsession, no abandon. He could have been a politician. He had thought about politics, quite a bit, in fact, when John Kennedy was alive. He had watched all the stuff on television. He had been angered and then touched by the Bay of Pigs. When he saw the replay of Kennedy's assassination in Dallas, he had wept, but he hadn't allowed anyone to see him weep. He could be president. Anybody could. All you had to do was be born in the damned country.

Or a poet. A painter maybe. Or a writer. What did it take

to say what you felt, except that he had never been in the habit of doing it. Oh, sure he had. He said what he felt all the time. You couldn't help that. But not really. Not when it counted. Not trying to find out what you truly felt and then saying that. He might have been anything if he had known what he felt.

He watched the naked buttocks of his son. He did not remember exactly what this Missy looked like. Something with brown curls and tits the size of oranges and a dimple in the chin. How many fathers have watched their sons do it? Not many, he thought. Yet it was nothing special. Up and down the street, around town, all over the world everybody fucked everybody. Nobody could be here unless everybody had gotten fucked.

"Right now, he must think he's stealing the moon," Charlie said. "I thought Jesus would throw me out of paradise, but it was worth it."

At the height of such an extraordinary event, Charlie was struck by the ordinariness of his life. He had made no contribution. He was for or against nothing. He had grown up. He had gone to school. He had married and produced children. He had obtained employment and made money. A good portion of money. And he spent the money. That was it. That was the sum of it. And stray pussy.

He stepped back from the car and looked down. He had an erection. He could not get to the front door, and David's peripheral vision might pick him up trying to open the gate to the backyard. Charlie turned and ran. He ran up the block and the dogs barked. He forgot about the fifty steps walking. He ran two hundred yards and collapsed onto somebody's agapantha. He lay there, panting.

He waited until his heart slowed and the dogs stopped barking. Then he walked home. The car was gone.

He opened the front door and went inside. A light was

burning in the living room. He could smell the roast Marian had cooked for dinner.

He went upstairs. Marian was asleep, the top sheet pulled over her nakedness. Charlie took off his sweats and crawled into bed. She didn't move. Running, he decided, had nothing to do with anything.

He lay thinking. David would get this Missy pregnant. There would be a big talk. Missy's parents would be there. Or was it just Missy's mother. He recalled that Marian had said Missy's parents were divorced. But somebody would want to keep the kid. David's face would be white and his eyes would beg to get rid of it. But somebody would want the kid. Missy's mother most likely. David didn't have a chance.

"Babies," Charlie whispered into the quiet dark.

* * *

When Vivian climbed the steps from the BART station, she was holding a red rose in her mouth. Her black dress fit like a sheath. Charlie laughed.

"You're crazy," he said, taking her arm.

"I hope so," she replied.

"I'm glad you have that coat. I don't want you showing off. I'll have to fight every bastard in town. Well, half of them anyway. The other half," and he waved his hand.

She raised a finger.

"Can't make jokes like that?" he said.

"You shouldn't. Not anymore."

"Everybody's sensitive."

"Everybody has rights."

"I remember when you could joke about anything. Jews. Spicks. Japs. Greasers. Queers. It didn't make any difference. It was OK."

"It's not the '50s anymore, Charlie."

"Is that what it is?"

"Nobody wants to be a joke anymore."

164

"Everything's serious."

"Not necessarily serious. People just want to be taken seriously."

"I was just happy to see you. I was just having fun telling you, that's all."

"I know. That's why I wasn't angry."

"I don't really mean that stuff. Queers can be queers. They can be queer all they want. I just don't like to see it, that's all. There are a lot of things in this city I don't like to see. A lot of what I see makes me mad."

"Me too."

"That's all."

"Let's start over," she said.

"What do you mean?"

"I mean I didn't want to sound so parental. I was upset."

He guided her across the street. "What's wrong?"

"I was attacked again last night."

"What?"

"Well, not exactly attacked. Just rotten eggs and vegetables thrown into the yard. Obscene phone calls. 'Hey, nigguh, a big white sausage gonna split yo black snatch wide open. Gonna make you drink white man's milk. Gonna be big, nigguh. Gonna be real soon now.' That's 1950, Charlie."

"Jesus H. Christ."

"Want to split my black snatch wide open, white man? It's yours, if you want it. All it costs is a nice dinner."

"Viv."

"You can go brag on all your white-assed friends how you had a nigguh woman. Treat you real fine, massuh. Give you long head. Give you long pleasure. Massuh. Oh, massuh."

The BMW was parked a block away and Charlie said nothing until they got to the lot. He opened the door for her and went around to the other side. When he got in, she was crying.

"Charlie," she said.

"There's a small place over on West 24th called Little Italy. Great zabaglione. Is that all right?"

"Charlie."

"You were right," he said. "It's not 1950. All that shit should have been finished a long time ago, but it's not. It's not finished."

"I'm a person. I'm a real person, aren't I, Charlie?"

"How could you ever say that? Coming from you. I don't believe you said that."

"No," she said. "I don't mean to those assholes last night. I don't have any trouble with assholes. But I'm just a woman, aren't I? I mean, a person."

"You're probably the most beautiful woman person I know."

"And just a woman person."

"A black woman person."

"Not because I'm a black woman person, though."

"No. You're just black."

"But that's not why."

"No."

"Any more than you're a white man person and that's why."

"I hope not."

"Just two persons."

"Yes."

"Two real persons."

"As real as anything. More real."

"How?"

"Together. More real together. Don't you ever talk that way to me again."

"I won't."

"Never again. I can't take it."

"I can't either."

"I don't know why it is, but it tears me up to have you do something like that."

"I won't again."

"You're just a person to me. A beautiful black person."

"You're a beautiful white person to me."

"I'm so glad," he said, "but I don't know why. I honestly don't know why."

"Don't you, Charlie?"

He stared out the windshield. Then he laid his head against the steering wheel. She put her arm around his shoulders. After a moment he raised his head.

"Please move out of that goddamn place."

"I am," she said. "I don't need all that. They frighten me, but I'm not scared of them. Do you understand?"

"Yes."

"I don't need to prove anything. I thought I did, but I don't really. I did all that a long time ago. And I don't need that shit anymore."

"Just please move. Right away."

"I'll get a condo or an apartment somewhere. Maybe even here in the city. It would be easy to be together then if I lived in the city. Would you like that?"

"Yes."

"No strings. Just to be together whenever."

"Shut up."

"OK."

"Just move."

"I'm starving," she said.

When they got to the restaurant, it was still early enough and the Friday night crowd had not arrived. They sat at a table in the back next to the grill. Charlie ordered garlic tomatoes and wine.

"I want to thank you for the thing with Kelly," he said.

"She's a good kid."

"Goodie goodie, maybe."

"No, just a good kid. It's tough being young these days. A lot of kids aren't doing it too well. Dope. Violence. It's hard growing up now. I wouldn't want to try it."

"The religion thing bothers me, I guess."

"It shouldn't. It's just a phase. I've seen others go through it."

"She clings to it and stops thinking."

"That's how I was with my husband. You make things into these little gods. That's how people are when they're scared."

Charlie looked away to the street so that he would not have to see her eyes. "I'm scared," he said. "A lot of the time. But I don't have any god."

"Sure you do. You make money."

"But I don't worship there."

"Maybe that's how you fool yourself. You kind of don't care and put down the whole thing, even while you're doing it. So you save something of yourself. But you ride to the temple every morning in a silver chariot. Gods don't have to be worshipped, Charlie. They can just be parked in the driveway."

"Is it always going to be like this with you?" he said, drinking the wine.

"Like how?"

"Like this. All the heavy-duty shit."

"What do the rest of your girls talk about?"

"C'mon."

"You do have other girls, don't you?"

"I don't have other girls."

"You have had, though."

"C'mon, Viv."

"What do they talk about?"

"They don't talk about anything."

"I bet they talk about the relationship. They talk about

168

when am I going to see you next and oh how good it feels and oh how lonely they are. All that lovey shit."

"You're a smart ass."

"A black smart ass."

"A smart smart ass. Why do you want to talk about other women?"

"Girls."

"I don't care about the guys."

"You don't?"

"What difference would it make?"

"It wouldn't. But you wouldn't care?"

"Sure I would care."

"Then say so."

"Goddamn it, Viv."

All the while she was smiling in a way that made him want her even more.

"Maybe we should talk about racism and greed and worshipping god. Those are good things to talk about. We'll just have love making here and there. And no lies. We shouldn't ever lie, Charlie. That's the most important thing."

"I don't want to lie to you."

"That's the biggest lie of all. You want to lie right now."

"I do not. What are you saying?"

"You want to believe there's something here. You want to give a name to it."

"There's something here. What are we doing, then?"

"Let's not categorize it or pigeonhole it or anything. Then maybe it will stay for awhile. Don't think you know what it is. You don't have to know it. I don't want to. It isn't anything. Just Charlie and Vivian having dinner. Charlie and Vivian being somewhere and going to bed."

"Charlie and Vivian making love."

"Making whatever."

"What's wrong with making love?"

"Nothing's wrong with it."

"Isn't that what we're doing?"

"That's the name people give it."

"You're scared, too."

"All the time."

"Are you scared of me?"

"No."

"Of what might happen?"

"Not in the least."

"Of what, then?"

"Of lying. And not knowing that I'm lying."

"You and me? Now?"

"No. Not yet. That's what I'm afraid of. Not yet. So don't tell me you love me. Don't ever say it to me. I don't want to hear something that you think you have to know about us so that it can go away. Truth doesn't go away. So let's just have truth with each other."

Charlie ordered the vegetables contadina and spaghetti and meatballs. The small cafe had filled. People were standing by the door, spilling out into the street. They were of that mixture one finds in the city, everything all scrambled and in costume. But there was a fair sense of the locals from the neighborhood along 24th. Beat up sneakers, Birkenstocks and unshaved legs. She told him about her childhood. He talked about his career.

"So how did you meet Ruth?" he asked.

"Believe it or not, it was because of running."

"For or against," he said.

"We were both in the Bay Cities Marathon. That's when I first came up from Fresno after the divorce. She caught my heel from behind and I went down. She dropped out of the race to give me a hand."

"Sounds pretty honest."

"That's how she was. She loved to compete, but all the

human values came first. Then we got into politics."

"You ran for office?"

"No. ERA. Fair housing. Day care. Toxic wastes. All those noble causes you become involved in because you're not getting enough."

"They say the success of the American businessman is in direct proportion to his lack of nookey at home."

"That's called compensation."

"Don't start." He filled her glass from a fresh bottle of wine. "So anyway."

"So anyway we became close friends. All those causes and things meant a great deal to Ruth. She used to say that the modern era was characterized by the growth of individualism and the loss of individuality. If the average person doesn't stand up and get counted, then we run the risk of being crushed by forces over which nobody seems to have any control. We have to make people stop doing things to each other. That's what she used to say. She loved this city, but it troubled her. All cities she'd been in troubled her. And I'm not sure why. Something about what happens when everyone presses together to use each other to make money. She got deep down under it. Most people just go shopping."

Charlie drank from his wine glass. Then he drank again. He felt something turning and turning.

"We did a lot of things together. Demonstrations. Sit ins. We had a lot of fun. I could kind of stay above it. I rather looked at it all from a distance."

"Because you were black."

"Yes."

"But she was a Jew."

"And she took it all very specifically. Figure that one out. You would have liked her, Charlie. She would have felt sorry for you at first, but she would have liked you too. She would have turned that cynicism around. Maybe she saw that in me

171

too. I never believed in the causes the way she did."

"You believed in her."

"Yes. I became more tolerant of people. Maybe that's what I needed. People tended to make Ruth sad."

"That's it," Charlie said.

"That's what?"

"About this place. I've never been able to put my hand on it, but that's just it. There's a sadness about this place." He sat forward. "Union Square. You see the people begging, with the head of a cat poking out from a dirty flannel shirt or a filthy- haired kid squatting between a ragged woman's legs. And the piece of cardboard. No place to sleep and no food. Please help. Or Hard times. Can you spare some change? And in Macy's and I. Magnin's and Neiman Marcus thousands of shoppers spending thousands of dollars on trivial things they don't need. Somebody with no legs playing a harmonica and strumming a guitar. A black man banging those tinny kettle drums. Thats what it is."

"Charlie," Vivian said. His voice was too loud.

"And then you feel anger. Why aren't the bastards off their asses and working somewhere instead of holding their children and mangy cats out for your pity and quarters? You begin to hate, hate the whole fucking thing. The whole presence of it. You hate being there and walking around and through it, the queers, the guy with a coat and tie going through the trash barrel on the corner of Geary and Post. The fucking leather jackets and the tourists in their bermuda shorts and Nikons and the teenagers with fourteen carat crucifixes dangling from their ears. Because it's the same fucking people week after week, holding out their scrawny kid or their scrawny cat. And the same fucking kettle drum player. And the same fucking cardboard sign saying the same fucking thing. Help me. Give me a quarter. Down on my luck.

172

"And then you shut it all off. You get blasé. You turn cold. You walk by it all and you don't hear it or smell it or see it or give a shit, it's just there like the buildings and the goddamned streets. It's just the goddamned city. And then something goes off down inside. You hear yourself way down. There's somebody crying. Something you heard a long time ago and had to shut off. And you want to scream because you're so goddamned sad and lonely for yourself. I hate this fucking city."

Charlie caught his breath. He felt as though he had run a hundred yards. The silence from the couples around him shed a pallor on the tables below and even reached the door, where people craned their necks and asked, "What is it?"

"I'm sorry," he said. "Jesus H. Christ."

"What for?" she asked, her back to everyone.

"For embarrassing you. I've had too much to drink."

"When you embarrass me, I'll let you know."

"I feel silly."

"Sure you do. That's how you feel."

"Smart ass."

"Pass me the meatballs."

When they got to the zabaglione, Charlie asked, "So where did our Ruth meet her Abraham?"

"Back East in school. He'd be damned if he'd go to Vietnam and she'd be damned if he would, too. Maybe that's where it all started for her. In those days Abe was idealistic as well. They'd be damned if anything. You know. Everybody was damned like that."

"Sure."

"Weren't you?"

"No. You want some more wine?"

"I don't want you to get drunk."

"Why not?"

"You might not remember what to do later."

173

He laughed. "I've never been so drunk I didn't know what was going on."

"You've never been really drunk, then."

"Not really. I guess I haven't. Have you?"

"Not really. I guess I always wanted to know what was going on, too."

"Is that a flaw in our characters, do you think?"

"Not wanting to get drunk?"

"No. Always having to know what's going on."

"I never thought of it like that."

"And then there's the other thing."

"What other thing?"

"Being afraid of not knowing what isn't going on."

"That's profound."

"Isn't it?"

"What does it mean?"

"Shit, I don't know. I wasn't paying attention."

Her chair was around next to his. He held her hand. He could smell the wine and garlic on her breath. He inhaled. There wasn't anybody else in the room, and he didn't want to be anywhere else or do anything else. It had been a long time since he had felt that way. He could only feel like that fishing alone on a trout stream in Montana.

"So anyway."

"So they came out here and knocked around a bit. Abe wanted to do research. You know. Eradicate cancer. Find a cure for something or other. Ruth got into human services. She never lost it. After awhile Abe started to lose it. Then it was gone."

"How do you know?"

"He started to worry about money. Everybody worries about money. You know what it costs to live around here. But Abe worried about it. He really did. Ruth had a bout of influenza. She got quite sick. Almost died. Abe went pretty

174

crazy about medical bills. All of a sudden he seemed to get scared. It was as though everything was up in his head before, but now something was happening to his body -- Ruth's body -- and he had to take care of it and fuck everything else. So he went to work for the Eisner company developing things that make a lot of money and pollute the environment. The ironic thing was that he started it because he loved Ruth and wanted to be sure she was all right. Then he just kept on with it. And that's when Ruth started drinking."

"You never mentioned that before."

"I never thought of it all together before. She wasn't an alcoholic. She could never run and do that. She just drank once in a while when she got to thinking. They were approaching middle age and Abe was inventing pesticides. It was tough on her. After all, she had watched him burn his draft card."

"That would make me mad."

"That's how I felt when Martin Luther King was murdered. But I got over it. Now I don't feel anything about it. You just go on. Whenever that shit comes on the tube, I shut it off. Jesse Jackson bores me."

"That's pretty astounding."

"Is it?" She patted his cheek. "We're supposed to be in the streets or singing hymns at the Baptist church. We're supposed to be so sensitive to social and political issues. We're supposed to be defensive."

"No, that's not it at all," he said. "What's astounding is I didn't even know the woman and I'll be goddamned if I don't keep on with it and get myself maybe into some trouble over it, but it doesn't seem to matter, I just have to keep on. And something's going on, all right. Safecon."

"What did you say?"

"The Safecon Project."

"I've heard that name," Vivian said.

"Where?"

"Once. Ruth mentioned it. Then she shut up."

Charlie looked at the bottle of red wine. He touched the label.

"I found out that Danilow is in Los Angeles for three days on business. How would you like to break the law with me? It might help us with Ruth's suicide."

* * *

The address on the card read 2432 Kensington Way. Charlie parked the BMW down the street and shut off the engine. He took a flashlight out of the glove compartment.

"Now what?" she said.

"You know the inside of the house pretty well, don't you?"

"I guess so."

"All we have to do is get in, then."

"Charles."

"You don't have to come along if you don't want."

"Oh, swell."

"Stay out here in the car. I'm going inside. It just seems the next logical thing, that's all."

"You want me to get behind the wheel and keep the motor running."

"I'm not justifying it. I'm just doing it. C'mon."

They went across the street and in behind some hedges. The wooden gate to the backyard was locked. He gave a hard pull. The screws tore. He waited. There were no dogs. Even the street lights were farther apart. An older neighborhood, it had not yet surrendered to the anxiety of the wealthy homes where he lived. However, because of the peculiarities of city planning, the house was quite near that same park he could see from his own driveway, just around the other side. Charlie looked up. The pale white of the moon lay upon the willow limbs hanging above the roof.

"What are you going to do?" Vivian said.

"Find a window. I saw it in a movie once."

"I'll lose my job if we're caught, you know."

"Wait in the car."

"Fuck you."

"I hope so."

They got into some piracantha before a window cut into four rectangular frames.

"This place must have been built in the thirties," Charlie whispered.

"They wanted a place like that," Vivian said.

"Reminds me of home."

"What home?"

"Where I grew up. We lived in a house like this in the valley."

"Roots," Vivian said.

"What roots?"

"They wanted a sense of roots."

"It's locked. I'll have to break it."

He knelt and switched on the flashlight.

"Charlie, I'm getting nervous. Suppose somebody's seen us."

"Nobody's seen us. Help me find a rock or a brick or something."

"But suppose we've been seen."

"Go wait in the car."

"Why do I like you so much?"

"It's my long dick. Here's something."

It was a metal sprinkler, one of the round kind with holes in concentric circles.

"It'll make a noise," she said.

"That was in the movie, too."

Charlie took off his jacket and wrapped the sprinkler head in one of the sleeves. He tapped an upper rectangle of glass.

The glass said, "Tunk." He struck hard and the glass broke. He pushed the shards away. Vivian was watching the back fence.

"This is crazy," she said. "Have you ever done anything like this before?"

"Never. See anything?"

"Nothing."

"We're lucky."

"So far."

"C'mon, I found the catch."

Charlie opened the window and brushed at the broken glass.

"Now what?"

"Now I'll shinny on in and then I'll help you."

"In this $500 dress? You shinny on in and then go open the front door. At this point, what difference can it make?"

"OK."

"This is a back bedroom. There's a hallway. Turn left and you'll see the front door. I'll go around now."

He pulled himself into the room and stood for a moment. There was a bed against the far wall, but it was a small bed. He could smell the house. There was the sense of being someplace unfamiliar and yet the sense of familiarity that comes from being a spy. He stepped into the hall, which had the shapes of photographs along the walls, and opened the front door.

"Now what?" Vivian asked.

"Now we start looking."

"What are we looking for?"

"Safecon."

"You don't expect to find that around here."

"He was working on Safecon when Ruth killed herself, wasn't he?"

"What are you saying?"

"He must have an office in the house, a desk at least. A guy like that takes work home."

"There's a room they fixed up in the basement. Ruth had a reading chair, too."

He switched on the flashlight and put his fingers over the lens.

"OK," he said.

She led him back down the hall. There was a door at the end. She opened it.

"These places always had basements," he said. "My place had a basement. I used to love to go down to the basement during the summer. That's how I got away from my old man."

"Charlie, this is all pretty scary. You're confusing me again."

"Go out in the car. Give a couple of toots if someone comes."

"I'm not going out to the goddamn car."

"I'm scared too. C'mon."

He led the way down the concrete steps. The air smelled of dry wood. There were no windows so he took his hand from the lens. On one side of the ten-by-ten room was a counter. Instruments hung above it. In the far corner were a desk and lamp. There was a computer on the desk. Next to that sat a cushioned chair and footstool. The desk and chair shared the lamp.

"Cozy," he said. "What's in the cupboards?" He opened one and found jars of jam and preserves.

"Ruth liked to put up things. Said it relaxed her. She even tried her hand at brewing beer. That's what the crock is for."

"All right," he said. "Let's go through this."

He opened the desk drawers, lifting things, putting them back.

"Do you know what we're looking for?" Vivian asked.

"Maybe files, records, information. Anything about

Safecon."

"Abe is pretty careful about company business. He wouldn't leave information or documents just lying around. He kept all the confidential stuff at work or locked into a safe upstairs."

"A safe."

"Don't tell me you want to break into that."

He laughed. "If only I had the talent." There were some papers and memos on the desk. He began shuffling through them.

"Charlie, I think I heard something."

"There isn't anything."

"But I heard something."

Charlie was staring at a piece of paper.

"Can we go now, please? Charlie?"

"Jesus H. Christ," he said.

She moved toward the steps. "C'mon." He held the paper. "What's wrong?" She walked back. "Charlie?"

He handed it to her. There was one word: Bredesen.

Vivian put the piece of paper on the desk. They stared at it.

"What does it mean?"

"How should I know?" he said.

"Did you ever meet him?"

"Never."

"He doesn't know you, then."

"Maybe now he knows me."

"But I don't think he wrote that. His letters were always very small and tight together. Those are all spread out and they lean."

Charlie bent closer.

"I want to go right now," she said. "I'm leaving."

She moved to the steps and he followed. Then he went back to the desk and put the paper into his pocket.

They hurried across the lawn.

"I'll be goddamn go to hell."

"What is it?" she asked.

"I was talking to myself." He opened the car door for her.

"What are you talking about, Charlie?"

"Those honky bastards," he said. "That's Harry Carpenter's writing."

CHAPTER EIGHT

Charlie wanted to run across the meadows far behind the ridges of Yellowstone or Yosemite.

He had driven through Death Valley once in the spring, and he had never forgotten. There was no one else on the road that day, and the sky was white-blue. For dozens of miles the earth was empty and dry, and then it turned upside down, like a magnificent stone, to reveal the fragments of something that had never lived.

Nothing was green. Even the cactus was sterile and pale against the dirt and rock. The car went down, down, everything getting dryer, the edge of sky indistinguishable from the horizon of land, and the solitude rose up and came into the car. It should have frightened him, but he had felt quiet. It had been quiet and beautiful.

He did not want to pass automobiles or houses. He did not want to see well-cared-for lawns. Or gas stations. Or pizza joints. He wanted the people gone. But he wanted the trees, the grass and sky. And animals. The animals had to be there, just as they always were, but without flea collars or raggy little sweaters or harnesses. When he was a kid living in the country, there had been all the space. The dogs roamed freely, there were no laws about it, and even though Tippy, his chow, had killed two dozen of old man Podesta's chickens one morning, the old man could have shot Tippy, but his father paid for the chickens and tied one around Tippy's neck, and that's how it was. So he ran in the park.

It was pleasant in the park in the afternoon. There was the light above the trees. In the shadows were shrubs and flowers. Paths went through the park. Here and there were benches and fountains. There were ponds with lillies and turtles and arched wooden bridges so you could look down through the olive green water at the orange and yellow carp. In the center of the park was a grassy space with a gazebo and miniature lake. There were canoes for the lake. In the summer you had to reserve them because they would only allow so many, but in the winter there was no need, and you would sometimes see a canoe on the water and a man in a heavy sweater and skull cap paddling a woman dressed in a down jacket, and the breath of the man was like smoke. They had band concerts in the summer, and if it was a large group, they used the gazebo, but sometimes they floated a platform out into the middle of the lake and the band played there and they used the special water proof lamps and sold tickets for charity. On a warm evening Charlie could hear the music drift through the window into the family room when he hit the mute button on the remote during the commercials.

It was a few blocks to the park. By the time he got there he felt the rhythm of his stride. Fifty paces running and fifty paces walking had lengthened to seventy-five, but there was no desire to push any harder. He had already dropped four pounds, and the blood pressure had inched below one hundred. He had taken it one night near the drug counter in Raley's, waiting until almost closing to avoid bumping into someone. The machines were supposed to be accurate. Dr.

184

Keh had said so. But he felt funny sitting there with his arm stuck into the gizmo next to the hand lotion and the tampons, and when the computerized lights came on, he looked around to see if anyone was watching. In good time the other sixteen pounds would be gone and the blood pressure would be below eighty. With a minimal but concentrated effort, he was saving his life.

When Charlie crossed that invisible line which separated the park from the city, when he was carried into the great oaks and the sycamores by the simple movement of his legs, he was struck by an odd sense of the familiar. As a boy he had lived beneath such trees, miles from town, where the stars revealed themselves and you heard the wind above the fields. Now, through the oaks and sycamores, he could see the city streets and the stucco shapes of condominiums and apartment buildings. He heard the sound of a basketball hitting a rim. Someone yelled, "Change the goddamned thing," and a radio came on. Years ago, somewhere in the '40s or even as late as the early '50s, the city fathers had decided to spare this remnant of a past civilization, and it had become surrounded by millions of tons of concrete and 1,000 square miles of blacktop.

Charlie turned into the park. There were trails that led deeper into what must have been an original wood. The benches disappeared and the fountains. The paths to the artificial lake were always maintained. Bicyclists used them. People on skates. But the trails had only pine needles and leaves, and though he knew that eventually all of this would butt up against a supermarket or a shopping center, still, as he slowed for his seventy-five paces walking, Charlie wanted to think he had found something young again.

Perhaps they weren't trails at all, not human trails. Animals made them, wandering down for water or salt. Deer had roamed here freely once. Even grizzly. There were still coyotes in the gullies beyond the housing developments. Sometimes a mountain lion appeared on Diablo. He had himself seen a fox one evening driving across the ridge from the Petrini's in Pleasant Hill. There was an occasional racoon or wildcat, and always twisted furry things lying along backroads leading out of town.

The response that he had to this regimen of exercise continued to surprise Charlie. He had expected to be bored. Others, speaking about running, warned of the plodding monotony and how the mind drifted to the soles of the feet. Long distance runners spoke of a vacuum, of an inertia of self. "I don't even look around," Randy Chisholm, who worked for a computer firm and hung out at the Cadillac Bar and Grill, said about something he called an "ultra."

Charlie couldn't help thinking. The physical act of quickening his stride from the business stroll he usually employed to the bouncing rhythm of an easy run, a run that, even after this short time, he already believed was connected to something more than health, seemed to trigger a mechanism inside his brain. Images went off. He remembered things and places. He even got hungry, a kind of hot, animal hunger, and water tasted better than beer.

He no longer believed that he might have a heart attack. It wasn't stress that he had been suffering from. It was more like sloth, a kind of fattened slow down of the metabolism of life. His heart had come under strain because it wasn't being used, that was all.

He had now arrived at a place that he did not recognize. The park had an odd shape anyway, as though too much had been contained by too little, and the result was a bulge here and there about the perimeter. One curve touched the freeway to the west. Another stopped at the landscaped backyards of designer homes to the north, while yet another simply disappeared into the foothills to the east. Charlie suspected that he had moved south, toward the flat line of trees that butted against the loading docks of supermarkets and department stores. There were cyclone fences here to discourage thieves and the users of spray cans, who might escape through the wood, but the fences also prevented access to the park by lawabiding citizens. As a result, the trees and shrubs, the plants and flowers were allowed to grow haphazardly. As it reached toward the walls and fences, the wood was at its most primitive.

Charlie stopped beneath a tangle of branches and limbs. The bushes were so thick that he could not see through them. There was a sweet smell in the air, as if something ripe had opened, and a humming sound, though it was too early for bees. In the shoats of light, irridescent particles floated. Something brushed his face and flew away.

An emotion occurred. He could only describe it as akin to mourning. The cathedral of shadow had perhaps inspired it, the sense that, at the center of the community in which he lived, something was lost, irretrievably. He was startled to find that the very edges of the leaves were trembling. He put his hand out. There seemed to be something to touch. When he stepped forward, an opening appeared. The undergrowth fell back.

Someone was standing there.

Charlie recognized him immediately. He was wearing a pair of grey cotton running shorts and a white tee shirt inscribed with the word Amherst. But it was the legs, those hairy Buster Keaton legs, that gave him away. He was holding a small, brown paper bag.

Charlie did not move. Neither did Buster Keaton. There seemed an inevitability about this. A heavy door slammed. They were quite close to the cyclone fence and the loading docks. Yet the shrubs were so thick they might as well have been in the jungle.

Charlie stepped forward and the man put his hand into the bag. Charlie moved again and the man began to jog in place. Then he broke into a run, coming straight for Charlie. At the last moment he veered away, and Charlie saw the same look in the eyes, as from the bottom of a well, but this time, just as the man flashed by, one of the eyes winked, directly at him. Charlie spun around and watched Buster Keaton disappear into the woods.

* * *

"You like it, white boy?"

"Will you cut that out," Charlie said.

She laughed and pulled the top sheet up to her chin.

"Nice?"

"Very. Now take the sheet off. You know I want to look at you."

"You never saw anything like this before, I'll bet."

"Never."

"I believe you."

"I wouldn't lie to you."

"Yes, you would."

"I would, but I won't. We have a deal."

"No lies."

"None. Ever."

"I'm beautiful."

"The most I've ever seen."

"No lie?"

"You're the most beautiful."

"It doesn't matter," she said.

"I'm not lying."

"It doesn't matter. Even if you do, it doesn't matter, because it's asking too much. I just don't want you to, that's all."

Charlie lay on his back and looked at the ceiling. A candle was burning on the nightstand. A yellow light filled the room. He could smell what they had done and, looking at the ceiling, he reached over and placed his hand upon her stomach.

"Maybe I'm grateful, too," he said.

She looked at him. "Did somebody give you something?"

"I think so," he said. "And I'm thankful."

"That's an odd way of putting it."

"I've been feeling odd. Have you ever reached a point when you just felt, well, odd? Different, I mean."

"When I got the divorce."

"I guess that would do it. I'm just grateful to you."

"Well, you're welcome."

"I like being inside you."

"I like having you there."

"Really, I do. But that's not what I mean. Not really."

She waited.

"Stupid, huh?"

"No," she said.

"I feel guilty."

"About this?"

"No, no. Of course not. I don't believe in that shit. I don't give a damn about that. Being like this just avoids hassle. All the words, if you know what I mean."

"Yes," she said.

"I don't know what it is. You go along. You have it pretty well figured out. There are things that are fucked, but it doesn't matter. It's like sweating. You have to. It's part of the game. So you take a shower and feel clean, and even if you sweat again, its just the game. Everybody sweats. So it doesn't matter. You got it made. And, after all, that's what they have soap for." He turned his head. "Is any of this making sense?"

"Keep talking," she said.

"I ask you not to, but I like it when you call me a honky

bastard or a white-assed sonofabitch. I know you don't mean it and I tell you to stop, but I like it. It gives me something. I can't explain it. It makes me feel good."

"Oh, God," she said, "do I detect that old trip you white folks have with us poor niggers. You beating yourself on the back with my pussy? You demeaning yourself and finding your soul?"

"That's not it, Vivian."

"Ain't no Jesus in my cunt, mistuh."

"That's dirty."

"There's soap right there in the bathroom. Go on and take a shower."

He removed his hand. The candle made a hissing sound and he heard the wax fall into the dish.

"No," he said. "No." He wanted to put his hand back. "I'm not used to saying how I feel and now you're pissed because I feel good, and I didn't mean anything like what you said."

"I'm not pissed."

"Is that a lie?"

"All right," she said softly. "So I'm hurt. Some."

"You make me feel my life."

"Oh, Charlie," she said.

"And it's not so much for being something as for not being something else, and I don't even know what. I look at the news and here are these kids from Asia or Africa or some damned place and they have these little bloated bellies and flies in their eyes and I don't feel as though I can help by sending in my sixteen dollars a month to adopt one of the little bastards. They say it's less than the cost of a cup of coffee a day to support some kid in India, and should I go around blowing air about racism? What the hell do they want? My life doesn't move in that shit. I see it advertised on television, but it might as well be detergent. That's what it is."

190

She raised herself on her elbows. Her breasts were enormous. It was amazing how enormous they were.

"Well, well," she said.

"Well, well, what?"

"Just, well, well."

"You see the black kids around town, what ones are here. They're wearing Reeboks and Vaurnets, for chrissake. The Mexicans make margaritas and sell used cars, and do you see any Cambodians or Laotians or Vietnamese except in restaurants? I'm not responsible for any of it. Why the hell should I be responsible? I'm just living my damned life. I pay my fucking taxes and live my life. That's enough. That's all any bastard does. Why is it my fault that someone I don't even know jumps off the Bay Bridge?"

She turned onto her side and faced him. "It certainly isn't your fault."

"That's what I mean. I didn't cause any of it, so it's not my responsibility."

"It isn't my responsibility either. It isn't anyone's responsibility. No one's to blame. Nobody should feel bad about it."

"They think life is something that's handed to you, when all the while it's something you have to pick up."

"Nobody ever handed me anything. I wouldn't take it if they did."

"You see? That's what I mean."

"If they hand you something, then you live your whole life that way, with your fucking hand palm up."

"I'm not mad about it."

"Nobody said you were."

"It makes me mad, though."

"What does, Charlie?"

"It makes me mad that it's all there and I'm here."

"Here?"

191

"That it's a whole world and it's not my world. I didn't make any of it. Not a damned bit of it. I just go about my business. Live and let live. That's the way it should be. I can't even get my own goddamned son through high school, and there they are with those leggy little animals and those snot nosed brats. Everybody has his hand out and so I'm supposed to drop in a buck or two, and then they feel something and I feel something, but there they all are anyway. I want another earthquake, an 8.5 on the Richter. I'd like to watch it all come down and then go out and look at the bay."

"That's the way Ruth used to talk."

"What?"

"She used to say she couldn't take it anymore. Then we'd go drive over to Bodega Bay or Mendocino. We'd go out on the beach and run. Sometimes we'd run until we couldn't breathe, and then we'd flop down in the sand and it would be better. It was like saving your soul, she said, being there alone and running that way."

Charlie sat up and put his feet on the floor. "Vivian, what's happening here?"

"I don't know, honey."

"The whole thing is amusing, right? That's the way it should be. But I'm not laughing. I'm not even smiling."

"Maybe you've got some nigger in you after all."

"What's that supposed to mean?"

"With all the raping and pillaging way back then, you never know. It would only take a drop or two. A little infection that took a long time to spread, that's all. Maybe it's Jewish. You have a little Jewish blood in you maybe."

"Maybe I wouldn't mind being black."

"You'd make a good nigger."

"I said black."

"See what I mean? Rabbi Bredesen."

"I wouldn't want to be a rabbi."

"You could be. You'd make a good rabbi."

"I'd much rather be black."

"OK."

"It's OK with you if I'm black."

"Be black. Then I can love you."

He sat on the bed, turned to look at her.

"How do I do it?" he said.

"I don't know. They have places to get a sex change. There ought to be a place to change color."

"Would you go to that place?"

"Why not?"

"They wouldn't have a place like that. Even if they could, I mean."

"Probably not."

"People would be changing back and forth. A guy could make a fortune, though."

"On how stupid people are. You could be president of the company."

"I don't want to be president of the company. And watch your lip."

"My, my, what have we here?"

"Besides, what would be the point of my becoming black if you became white?"

"No point."

"So here we are."

"Like an old movie."

He put a hand on her leg. "I like black and white movies. I like them better than color movies. Most of the actors I ever loved are dead anyway, the ones I went to see as a kid. Everything is broken apart, scattered all around. In technicolor."

She sat beside him on the edge of the bed.

"Charlie, when are you going to pull out of this?"

"That bad, is it?"

193

"I've watched you sink deeper and deeper. It seems all out of proportion."

"It does, doesn't it?"

"I'm sorry, but it does."

"Yes," he said. "Like that shit in your front lawn."

"Don't start that."

"I almost envy you having your burnt lawn and all."

"That's crazy."

"Not really. It's something. You have a center. It wouldn't be anything otherwise. It would be a prank, something by a bunch of drunk kids. But it isn't. There's a whole meaning there. It breaks across everything. You're all there. If they had that place to change color, I would go there and be black. Then I could have it too. Even if you didn't love me, you would anyway."

"Nigguh, you crazy."

"No, no."

"You want white folks hatin' and hurtin' you."

"No, suh."

"That's whut's there, nigguh. That's whut's waitin' fo you."

"Where's the doah. Show me the doah."

"You go in there, you can't never come back. You black, then you black."

"Praise de lawd."

"You silly goddamn white-ass nigguh. The whole nation wanna be white and you, you wanna be black. Why you wanna be black?"

"'Cause then, sister, then maybe I could love you."

She stared at him. Her eyes filled. "You sonofabitch. You crazy sonofabitch."

"It's tough to find out you don't belong to anything," he whispered. "That you don't believe in anything. Oh, I live someplace. It just happens to be here. Someday I may live

194

somewhere else, when I get promoted or divorced or fired. I have a hometown. One of those small towns in the valley. But I don't go back. I'm afraid to go back. I don't have a home. I have a house. I live in it with a bunch of people I call my family. The place is empty during the week. It's like a church. We're in there together sometimes on Sunday."

She put her arms around him. "Come here," she said. "C'mon down here. Poor white man. Poor, poor white-ass nigger."

He lay beside her. His body looked faded or bleached. He closed his eyes and ran his hand down the center of her back. There was a ditch, a lovely long ditch. The skin was smooth and tight. He moved his fingers into the ditch and followed it to the base of her spine. Then he spread the fingers over her hip and down to her legs. Her legs were firm and muscled. Runner's legs. He opened his eyes. Her brown flesh absorbed the candlelight.

Charlie did not want to make love to her. Of course, he wanted to make love to her, but not that way, not again, not just now. He wanted to hold her. He wanted to look at her. He wanted to touch her and above all to hold her, but that was enough, more than enough. She moaned a little and he held her tighter. He wanted her to know it was enough. He did not understand why but it was. She softened a little and he felt her relax. He held her and something was gone. It wasn't desire. He wanted her, but he wanted to hold her more. It was something else. It was gone. So he held her. She was heavy against him. Maybe she was asleep. With his head over her shoulder, it was difficult to tell. He watched the candlelight along her hips and legs. Maybe she was asleep. He would like it if she were asleep. He held her and closed his eyes. She was soft and warm and asleep against him. "Jesus H. Christ," he said. "I don't have a hard-on."

He must have fallen asleep himself because the whirring

of the phone made him jump. Vivian rolled away and sat up.

"I won't answer it," she said.

"What do you mean? Why not?"

"Nobody I know calls after ten. I won't answer it."

"It's those bastards."

"I'll unplug the phone."

"I'll answer it," Charlie said.

"No," she replied and picked up the receiver from the nightstand. "Hello," she said. She listened only a moment and then set the receiver down. Her face was not a lovely dark brown but a muddy grey.

"Vivian," he said.

She unplugged the phone.

"Viv."

"I'll have it disconnected in the morning. That's that. No more. Next time I get an unlisted phone. I don't have to listen to shit. It seemed amusing at first. But it's shit. They're scum. That's all they are."

"You should have let me talk to them. I'd have told the bastards off. Maybe hearing my voice would put them back a little."

"No, Charlie, no." She was trembling.

"Wait a minute," he said, taking her arm. "What is it?"

"In fact I'm getting out of here tomorrow. I'll find an apartment or something, turn this damned place over to a real estate broker. You were right. I should have gotten out of here right away. Well, I will, now."

"That's fine," he said, "fine." He put his hand under her chin, but she would not look at him. "What is it?"

"Maybe you should go now," she said. "It's getting late. Won't your wife wonder?"

"Sometimes I stay in the City if I work late. So I worked late. What is it?"

"Go home, honey. Please."

196

"What did they say?"

Her eyes held the opaque distance of terror.

"They wanted to talk to you," she said.

Charlie felt a tiny motion at the back of his neck. He looked at the far wall, where the candle was making vague corrugations in the curtains. There was an impulse to throw on his clothes and get the hell out. It would be better all the way around if he got out. What business was it of his? Wasn't there enough to think about? But he didn't move. He watched the curtains.

"Plug the phone in," he said.

"No, Charlie."

"Plug it in."

"I'll get out of here tomorrow and then it will be over."

"You're leaving tonight. You're not staying here alone another night."

"They wouldn't do anything, Charlie. They're just talking. They're sick, that's all."

"That's why you're leaving. I'll take you to a motel. Plug it in."

"All right, all right," she said. "We'll get dressed. We'll go right now."

"Plug it in first."

"Charlie, I don't want you to. You don't want to hear it, honey. You don't want to hear that."

"I don't want to hear anything. I want to say a few words. That's what I want."

He stepped around the bed and snapped the cord into the base of the phone. The phone was already ringing. He lifted the receiver.

"Bastards," he said. "Dirty scumbag, coward bastards. Shit, goddamn cowards. Sonsofbitches," he said. "Sonsofbitches." He couldn't think.

He was spitting into the mouthpiece. Vivian had both

hands to her face. He looked at the wall. His legs were trembling.

"Niggerman," a voice said.

"You scum!" Charlie shouted. "You fucking lousy scum!"

"Niggerman," the voice said. "Hey, niggerman. You think that's special. You think that's somethin' sweet. You got disease, Niggerman. You got real disease."

In a sudden rush of reason Charlie said, "Listen. Leave her alone, see? She hasn't done anything to you. Just leave her alone."

"You fuck a nigger," the voice said, "you ain't clean. We got a lot of soap here, niggerman. A lot of good white soap."

Charlie squeezed the receiver. "You lousy shit. Your mother had an abortion and you're what's left." He jerked the cord from the base of the phone. He looked at Vivian. "Get dressed," he said.

* * *

Charlie entered the park. The plop plop of his slow running echoed in his ears. The afternoon was pale. Storms were coming. Something had opened above the northern ice. That stream of air, which could cover the entire Pacific in one great bow, had dropped. The wind above California was chilled.

He ran easily beneath the oaks and sycamores and turned south. The blacktop disappeared. The pine needles crunched beneath his sneakers. Finally the shrubs grew close and thick. He stopped before the opening. His heart was pounding. He took a step, then another.

Buster Keaton was in the clearing. When Charlie came forward, Buster sat down.

Then Charlie was standing above him. "Who are you?" he asked.

"A mass murderer," the man replied.

Charlie looked at the clutter of branches and shrubs that

198

hid the cyclone fence. There was no escape that way. And he effectively blocked the opening behind him.

"You're a mass murderer then."

"That's what I said."

Charlie sat down.

"Well, that sounds like interesting work."

"Oh, it is," the man said.

"How many have you. . .you know?"

"Two dozen," the man said. "That I know of."

Charlie whistled.

"Not bad, huh?"

"It's funny, though. I don't remember reading any stories in the paper about any. . ."

"Remember the one last spring? The woman they found under the Antioch Bridge with her wrists cut? That was my work. And the one who turned her Volkswagen Beetle in between the front and rear sections of an eighteen wheel tanker truck on 580? That was mine. And how about the Berkeley sophomore who went into the chemistry lab and swallowed a glass of formaldehyde? Mine."

"You kill only women?"

"Most of them deserve it, wouldn't you say?"

Charlie thought about it and was inclined to agree. Buster's face seemed calm enough. There were no signs of strain around the eyes, which were set back rather far into the face. The sandy hair was receding above the temples, though there was a curl that dropped over the forehead. The lips were thin but parted and relaxed. If Buster was mad, it was with the clarity of the sane.

"You do this for a living?" Charlie asked.

"You think I'd do it for nothing?"

"I suppose not."

"There's big money in mass murder."

"Really."

"Big money. You just can't let them know you're doing it, that's all."

"I see."

"No, you don't. I've killed women in most of the major cities in America. But do you think they know I'm a mass murderer? They just have all these unsolved cases in all these cities. I've killed three in New York alone, that I know of. Chicago. St. Louis. A couple in San Francisco."

"You get around."

"It's easy. There's a trick to it."

"I supposed there would be."

"Actually, it's a secret. But I promised I wouldn't tell."

"Promised who?"

"You see. There I go already. I shouldn't even have told you it was a secret."

"I wouldn't say anything."

"Yes, you would. You would have to."

"So how can they not know you're doing it?"

"They all think I'm helping them, of course."

"You're helping them."

"Yes, of course. That's the whole point. At first I really was. Then that became the trick."

"You really want to tell me, don't you?"

"Yes, I do."

"Why? Why particularly do you want to tell me?"

"After a time you have to. That's the weakness of a mass murderer. After awhile you have to tell."

"But why me?"

"You run, don't you? I've seen you running."

"I've recently started running, yes."

"I run. All the time now. So that's the thing. And you seem interested. More than interested."

"In running."

"In running, of course. If you don't run, you die."

"It was your heart too?"

"My heart too?"

"Your blood pressure. It was my blood pressure."

"It wasn't my heart. It was something far below my heart."

"I don't get it."

"I don't either. But it's way down there. I run for hours sometimes and I'm at the point of exhaustion and then I feel something. I'm so tired I can't even think and then I feel it, way down there. I have to get worn out and then it's there, a little piece of something that hasn't been used."

"That's sad."

"Oh, it is. It is. Very sad."

"The sadness of the mass murderer."

"Yes. That's it. You get it."

"No, I don't."

"Me too. But that's it. I get to that place. I'm so exhausted and I'm there, and this little thing comes up, right from the bottom, and it's so beautiful. You see? Can you believe that at that point anything could be beautiful? But it is. I run for it. I run until I almost can't run. There has to be something beautiful at the bottom or I couldn't run at all."

Charlie looked at the man's eyes. An emulsion had formed, swelling into the corners.

"I'm sorry," he said.

"Yes," Buster said. "I know you are. You don't understand and you're sorry, and that's the best part of it. You're lucky, when it's just your heart."

Charlie looked up. Above the canopy of limbs a grey sky hung. It was one of those vague skies of winter. Perhaps cloud or maybe fog, mixed with the smoke of factories and the exhaust of engines. If nothing moved against it, a plane or a flag in the wind, even a bird, you might believe you lived at the bottom of the sea.

201

"Then why did you become a mass murderer?"

"No one becomes a mass murderer," Buster said. "There just comes a time and you are."

"You started out as something else, then."

"Everyone starts out as something else."

"You're not helping me."

"I know. That's the whole point."

"This is crazy."

"I'm afraid so."

Charlie looked at the sky.

"I should run along."

"That's funny."

"I wasn't trying to be funny."

"It's still funny."

"Well. . ."

Buster took a paper bag from under his sweatshirt and set it on the ground.

"I hope you won't run along. I'm not trying to be confusing. It's just that when someone makes a suggestion, a rather tenuous suggestion, about your life as a mass murderer, you have to think about it, that's all."

"Are you talking about me?"

"No."

"That's confusing."

"I suppose it is."

"Then, are you going to keep on with it?"

"My career, you mean."

"Yes."

"I don't know. What else is there?"

"You don't like it, do you?"

"No, I don't like it."

"You'll get caught one day, don't you think?"

"That was the suggestion."

"Well, what's the point? The whole crazy thing. If you're

a mass murderer. . ." This time Charlie couldn't help smiling. "I mean, if you're really a mass murderer, what's the point? You'll be found out."

"Time. I guess that's the point."

"Time for what?"

"Running?"

"You're asking me?"

"I suppose."

"How would I know?"

"You're a runner, aren't you? And you're interested. More than interested. That's what it seems."

Charlie stared at him. He didn't know whether to laugh or get mad. Buster was half his size.

"Hell, I could turn you in," he said.

"I know," said Buster. He lifted the bag. "That was the suggestion."

"Well, why don't we stop?" Charlie asked.

"Stop?"

"This. The game."

"There's no game."

"C'mon. I've gone along. What's the point? Who are you anyway?"

"I've confessed. I've told you of my crimes. That's who I am."

"A mass murderer."

"Yes."

"That nobody knows about."

"Some know."

"Really?"

"Yes."

"But they do nothing."

"They do nothing."

"A mass murderer and they know and do nothing."

"Yes."

"Well, a joke's a joke, but this is nuts. I'm leaving." He stood up. Buster stood too, clutching the bag.

"You mustn't go, not yet."

"Say," Charlie said. He clenched a fist.

"You see," Buster said, his face as grey as the sky, "the suggestion is that you know or could know, could come to know, out of your interest, and now I've told you, so what will you do?"

"You're crazy," Charlie said.

"You must do something. That's the point. You don't know, but you must do something. I think that's admirable. It really is." Charlie turned and Buster put his hand into the bag.

"What the hell are you talking about?" Charlie asked, stopping.

"How it's possible to not know and to feel compelled to do something anyway. As you're doing. It's admirable. It speaks of something inside, of something that isn't lost. I know about that, you see. I know all about getting lost. There's no one more lost than a mass murderer."

He stood facing him. There was a pain in Buster's eyes, like the eyes of a man at the bottom of a well, and Charlie looked into them. "Say, what is this?"

"What this is, is a suggestion," Buster said. "A suggestion that takes it away from mass murder, that makes it just murder, you see? It's not hard to be a mass murderer. You might think so, but it isn't. It's the easiest thing in the world to kill people from a distance. So now it's a matter of survival, and it all comes down to just one person, someone you have to look at, someone you have to remember, and that's why it's so hard, so damned hard."

Charlie's eyes opened wide.

"Now you understand a little," Buster said. "I see that you do. It's terrible when it becomes personal. We're not ready for it." Buster's lip was trembling. "She tried to tell me. It was

204

that way all those years ago. It all mattered once. But you forget. If you don't stay next to it, you can forget. But she never forgot, not me or how it was. Her death was my best work, wouldn't you say? Not like the rest, of course. But my hand was on it. It was definitely the work of a skilled mass murderer."

Charlie's mouth was dry. He stepped back.

"If only you had known then," Buster said. "If your concern had been found there on the bridge that morning, things might have been different. You were behind her. You could have run to where she was. Taken hold of an arm or a sleeve. Something. Stopped her. Just a little more time, that's all. But then we wouldn't be here, would we?"

"You're. . ."

"Yes, Mr. Bredesen."

Abe Danilow moved and Charlie sprang. His shoulder thumped Abe on the chin. The bag dropped and the gun spilled out. Abe fell and Charlie sprawled across him, swinging his arms. A fist struck something soft.

Charlie wrestled the small man, squeezing Abe's neck in the crook of his arm. Danilow twisted free and Charlie threw him onto his back, knocking the wind out of him. He hit Danilow in the face.

Charlie sat on Danilow's chest. Blood came out of the small man's face. Charlie hit him. His fist was red and he hit Danilow again. It was all right and he raised his arm and Danilow was smiling. Charlie looked at him. Blood was coming out of Danilow's mouth and nose. It was all over his sweatshirt. Some was on Charlie's pants. Danilow's teeth were shiny and red. And he was smiling. Charlie looked. Then he hit him. He hit him until there wasn't any more smile.

CHAPTER NINE

Charlie did not put on the driving gloves the following morning. The steering wheel of the BMW was cold. The leather seat was cold too. He could see his breath. The car had an excellent heater. It was the first thing he started after the engine.

He left the driveway, and when the windshield began to film, he opened the vent. By the time he made the turn onto Treat, he was shivering. He would have been listening to the traffic report as well. With heliocopters overhead and guys with cellular phones calling in, KCBS rode point against bottlenecks, stalled big rigs, oil spills, collisions and death. But Charlie drove in silence.

He got onto the freeway and stayed in the right lane.

"Safecon," he said.

Charlie felt the metal of the car. It was thick around him, all the weight of it going effortlessly toward the Caldecott. He always enjoyed the feeling. It was how the metal dovetailed together, all of it painted so many times, all of the heavy manufacture of it, the power steering and the gears taking it along, while inlaid upon it, artfully, all the leather and the smell that had been produced in Germany so that he could be the owner here in Walnut Creek.

He was driving too slowly, even for the morning commute. Cars stacked up behind him. Drivers jammed their horns. They took chances to get around, swearing and gesturing. He sat forward, both hands on the wheel. The tip of his nose was cold, his toes and fingers. He stared at the road and crept through the turn toward Lafayette.

There is a confluence here. New lanes rise at the left from the center of town. To the right other traffic appears, as though disgorged. The far right lane becomes the center of the freeway.

Charlie gripped the wheel. He could not get into focus. He began to move to the right without showing a blinker and heard a squeel of brakes. He moved again, drifting, and found himself looking at the grass and pines growing from the hills. He had gone onto the paved shoulder.

"I can't do this," he said.

He stopped and shut off the engine. Behind him vehicles began to accordion. They drew up like playing cards, their bumpers almost touching, around the curve toward Ygnacio Valley Road. They stacked up at Treat Boulevard and then beyond. They crept by, staring at Charlie. Charlie sat gripping the wheel. He was watching the pines grow from the hills.

Finally, red and blue lights flashing, a highway patrol officer found his way to Charlie's BMW. He tapped on Charlie's window. Charlie looked at the officer.

"Roll the damned thing down."

Charlie complied.

"What's the problem here?" the officer said.

"I don't know," said Charlie.

"Are you all right?" the officer said. "You feel all right? You look sick."

Charlie put a hand to his forehead. He was sweating. "I

don't know." He thought a moment. "I'm all right. Sure, I'm all right."

"You'll have to move the vehicle," the officer said. "Get off the freeway."

"I'm all right."

"You're going to cause an accident. Can you drive?"

"I'm all right, Officer. Really I am."

"Follow me," the officer said.

The patrol car moved around Charlie. Charlie started the BMW. At the first ramp the officer turned off the freeway and pulled into a gas station. Charlie stopped alongside.

"May I see your license?" the officer said.

Charlie took it out of the wallet.

"Mr. Bredesen, if you're not feeling well, we can have someone come and get you."

Charlie read the brass plate over the man's pocket. "I got distracted, Officer Brooks. You understand how it is. Things get going. That's why I pulled over. I'm all right now."

"You have to pay attention, Mr. Bredesen. That's how people die out there. If you don't pay attention, you could kill somebody. You wouldn't want to be responsible for someone's death, would you, Mr. Bredesen?"

Charlie looked into the man's deep blue eyes. In the early morning there seemed to be a tiny fire burning in each of the irises.

"No," he said. "No one's death."

The officer did not blink, but fixed his eyes on Charlie.

"No," Charlie said.

The officer stood erect and looked out at the rows of automobiles hurtling by above him. "I want you to rest here a few minutes. Go into the bathroom, wash your face and hands. If you're OK, go on ahead. If not, go back home. Understand, Mr. Bredesen? Life is something you pay attention to."

"Yes," Charlie said.

The officer bent down and looked through the window. The tiny red fires burned Charlie.

"Have a good day, Mr. Bredesen."

Charlie stared through the windshield at a rack of tires placed against a low stone wall. There was a metal sign above the rack that said Union. Above the sign was a hill with pine trees and shrubs.

Charlie went into the bathroom. He splashed water onto his face. He dried his face with the paper towels. He stared at himself in the rectangular mirror. He went outside.

He looked at the BMW. It was shiny and new. The metal gleamed. Even the wiper arms gleamed. He had paid a lot of money for it.

He walked around to the driver's side. His reflection walked with him.

"I can just go home," he said, standing beside the car. "I can't do that."

Charlie got into the car and started the engine. He backed out of the station and drove up onto the freeway.

Lafayette went by and Orinda. The lanes lifted toward the Caldecott. Charlie stayed to the right and managed to maintain speed. The window was down and he was sweating.

There were three tunnels through the mountain, and in the morning they opened the center tunnel to the westbound commute. If it was a lucky morning, one with no accident, the traffic moved at a crawl the last half mile or so. He found himself hoping for crushed vehicles to be spread across the freeway. He would have liked to stop there in the cold mist and shut off the engine.

Instead, like gigantic centipedes, the automobiles connected in the two lanes to left and right. Charlie found that he could not make a decision. The barrier post came toward him, wrapped in steel. Either tunnel would take him to where he was going. But the barrier was a choice too. He blinked his eyes. The traffic left him on either side. He wanted to turn the wheel. He knew he could turn the wheel. He heard horns and stepped on the brake. The BMW came to a halt and the front bumper tapped the barrier.

Charlie sat looking at the mountain rising above him. All along the lanes behind him cars were coming to a stop. Slower than a man might walk, they crept near him, their drivers amazed and angry. Charlie put the BMW into reverse. He got into traffic and the tunnel swallowed him.

When he emerged at the other end, there was Berkeley and across the bay, the sullen, tall buildings of the financial district.

Things went a little better maneuvering the last few miles before the turn down to the bridge. But as he reached the toll plaza, his hands began to sweat. He drew up to the metered lights. When it was his turn to go, he killed the engine.

The vehicles began the ascent to the Yerba Buena anchorage. Charlie hugged the far right lane. More than once his tires touched the steel rail. "No," he said. When he got to the Yerba Buena tunnel, he was shaking.

He approached the place where Ruth had jumped. He was in the far right lane. The place was on the other side. Every day he had driven across and every day he had looked. They had been painting and there was a rust colored stain where she had gotten out of the car. She had stood just there. He was coming up on it. He slowed. Horns blared. He heard the screech of tires.

"No," Charlie said.

He stopped. The wind was whipping the bridge. He opened the door into traffic. He stepped through the lanes of stunned drivers to stand where Ruth had stood. He put his hands on the steel rail.

The water was an amazing blue. The surface was a

corrugation of blue. The wind pushed the corrugation along. So softly did it happen that the bridge seemed to be moving.

"Jesus," Charlie said. "Jesus H. Christ."

Then he threw up.

* * *

From his office window the bay had that color you might find on a picture postcard. The wind had blown the fog away. It had blown the clouds away too. A brilliant transparency lay upon the Berkeley hills. In that place where Ruth had disappeared the water was shadowed by the bridge.

Charlie stared at the water. He had been staring for some time when there was a knock at the door.

"Well, old boy," Frank said.

Charlie stood at the window. He did not turn. Frank shut the door and took a few steps. "Here it comes," Charlie said to himself.

"Janet was away from her desk. I saw your car in the stall. You've picked up a nasty scrape along that right front fender."

Charlie said nothing.

"They can rub it right out, though. I had a scratch on the GEL. The shop got it right out. Don't know how they do that. A little paint. Good as new."

Frank was standing at the window. He looked at the bridge. Then he looked at the water. Charlie could smell Frank's cologne.

"I'm sorry, old boy," Frank said.

Charlie turned. Frank was wearing a navy blue suit with a fine grey pinstripe. The tie was red with tiny chevrons of grey and blue. He looked at Frank's wingtips. Everything was new.

"Why would you be sorry?"

Frank's face reddened just enough to complement the tie. "I think it's appropriate," he said. "It's a tough thing, after

212

all."

"Tough? More for her than for me."

"She had her heart set on it, then."

"What heart?"

"Marian, of course. Her disappointment."

"I'm talking about Ruth Danilow. That's where she went into the water." He pointed.

Frank took a step to the side.

"They never found her body, you know. They dragged for it. I watched them. But it's gone. It may be off somewhere. The currents. But if you ask me, I don't think it's left. It's still out there floating beneath the bridge."

Charlie's lips were trembling. Frank watched him out of the corner of his eye.

"That's what I'm sorry about, Frank. What are you sorry about?"

"Listen, Charlie."

"What are you sorry about?"

"Haven't you seen Carpenter?"

"There's a message on my desk. I haven't gone up. That's what you're sorry about?"

"Jesus, I thought you knew. I wouldn't have come barging in here if I thought you didn't know. I never would have done that."

"So that's that."

"I'm so sorry, old boy."

Charlie stared at the bay. There was a yellow light rising from the surface. The light whitened the shadows under the bridge.

"Who?"

Frank shifted his weight. "Carpenter and the old man had a big conference. A lot of names went around. The whole team is qualified. You know that. Almost like drawing straws. Anyone could have gotten it. That's how close it was. So it doesn't mean all that much in the long run. Maybe, anyway."

"Congratulations, Frank."

Frank unbuttoned his coat. "If you could have kept your mouth shut, but the perception was that you wouldn't. I mean, you're a company man, and yet you're not. That was the notion. But I don't like thinking this thing comes on a windfall. I'm damned qualified, Charlie. You know I am. I'll be a damned good president. I'll give 100 percent. That's all I've ever done. I deserve it, as much as you or anyone. But I'm sorry. I really am. I don't understand, but I'm not complaining. Quite frankly, I thought you had the whole thing in your hip pocket."

"I'll give you quite frankly. You want to hear quite frankly? I don't give a damn."

"Charlie, what in Christ's name has gotten into you? That's dangerous talk."

"That's not dangerous talk."

"Your attitude, Charlie. That's what's dangerous. What's been happening to your attitude?"

"I'll give you dangerous. You want to hear dangerous?" He tapped him on the shoulder. "Safecon. Quite frankly, old Frank, what the hell is Safecon?"

"I don't know anything about it. I don't want to know."

"Ruth Danilow knew."

"What? What do you mean?"

"She knew something. Her husband was working on it. She knew all right. Tell me, Frank."

"I don't ask."

"You know about it?"

"In the old man's company. Before the merger. It's over now."

"How do you mean, over?"

"Terminated. The operation is terminated. That's that."

"That's what?"

214

"It was only one operation. Eisner Corp had all kinds of things going. You worked with the old man. How is it you never knew about it? Didn't you study the company?"

"Of course I did. I never came across Safecon. Maybe they didn't want me to know. But you know, Frank."

"I didn't ask." He looked at the door.

"No, you wouldn't."

"I believe in this company, Charlie."

"Loyalty is a good thing, Frank. It's an appropriate response."

"You could do with a little more loyalty."

"And so you could be trusted with certain confidences."

"Listen, Charlie."

"Confidences, Frank. They wouldn't have to make assumptions, as they did with me."

The collar of Frank's shirt was damp. He wanted to go to the door but went to the corner of the room and stared at the bridge.

"The old man always liked you. That's the thing, Charlie. People like you. But you don't commit yourself and they end up leaving. You were always so lucky. I couldn't understand how you got along. But people like you. It takes more, finally. I tried to tell you that. I was right all along. It's loyalty. It's committment. No matter what. Luck runs out. It's not always a passing game. If you're not truly dedicated, luck is not enough. Even if they like you."

It was a long speech. It was the longest speech Charlie had heard him deliver. He looked at Frank, wilting in his grey pinstripe, and a feeling came over him. He had never experienced such a feeling before. Someone he knew filled him with disgust.

He took a step. "All right," he said.

"I'm keeping my nose out of it. I don't even mention it. That's what got you into trouble with the old man, Charlie.

215

It's none of my business. I'm concerned about the new firm. That's all I care about. Eisner Corp doesn't exist anymore. It's been dissolved. Forget it. If you want to know my opinion, you shouldn't go around asking fool questions when you're told not to."

Charlie was standing next to him. He looked into Frank's eyes. They were lizard's eyes. "All the wash is on the line, then. So hang the rest of it out. I have a right."

"I don't know anything. I wasn't told about the operation. Nothing."

"Goddamnit, I don't want to know about the operation. What was it? What was it for? They told you that."

"Yes."

Charlie waited.

"Birth control."

"Christ."

"There were problems, but whatever they were, it's all taken care of. It's finished. So it doesn't matter, does it? All that matters is the company. That's what we should care about."

"Birth control," Charlie said,

"That's what I know," said Frank. "Nothing else."

They stood at the window. A freighter was sliding beneath the bridge. Its decks were filled with long, rectangular crates. There was Japanese writing on the crates.

"Something happened," Charlie said.

"Of course something happened."

"Something went wrong. Really wrong."

"Projects are abandoned all the time. There were problems. It wasn't profitable. It was dropped. That's all."

"Something," Charlie said, watching the feighter. "Something catastrophic."

"You're being melodramatic. This suicide thing. I can't believe you've let it get to you like this. You and Marian again, is that what it is, old boy?"

"Murder," Charlie said, staring at the flattened wake the freighter had left beneath the bridge.

" What?"

"Mass murder."

"You're crazy."

"And she knew. Right along, she knew."

"Charlie."

"Her husband was into it and she knew."

"You need a doctor."

"Dead babies," Charlie said.

Frank stared. Charlie watched the bay. He had read somewhere that it had taken a while for the Spanish to discover it. The neck into the harbor is small, and all the time, sailing up and down the coast, the Spanish had gone right by it in the fog. It must have been something then, just the emerald hills and the blue water of the bay to the north and south. No bridges. No buildings. No people. It must have been something. He would have given a leg to have seen it that first time.

"I can't talk to you."

"That's all right."

"Maybe you should take some time off. You worked hard on the Eisner deal. Take a trip. Go down to Rio. Go to Caracas. Puerta Vallarta. Take a cruise. You deserve it."

"The sonofabitch. The dirty old sonofabitch."

"Time away. That's what you need. For you and Marian. Ease things out. Something's happened. It's becoming destructive."

"Destructive?"

"Hurting yourself, Charlie. Here, with the company. Can't you see it?"

"Who wants to be president? I don't want to be president. I never wanted to be president."

"There's no reasoning with you."

"Reasoning."

"This company is our life."

Charlie stood at the window. Such a consideration had never entered his mind. That a life could be wrapped up, that it could be summarized in a few words seemed preposterous. There was always so much of it. It had so many directions. To have it all be one thing and so small a thing terrified him. He put his hand against the glass. It covered his image reflected upon the water.

Frank walked behind him. "Yes. So think about it." He went to the door. "By the way, I haven't told you. Julie and I are getting married again. We decided last night. I thought you should know."

Charlie removed his hand.

"No comment?" Frank said.

"Why?"

"Why are we getting married?"

"Why should I know?"

Frank came back a step. "It seemed a logical thing."

Charlie looked at him. "There is a logic to it, isn't there?"

"You don't think it a bit strange or anything? We have been apart for years."

"It seems logical, Frank. Like you say."

"We remained friends right along. Went to dinner, the theater. There are actually many things we have in common. We know each other so well. We couldn't live together. I think we can now. We'll leave each other alone. You know what I mean. People should leave each other alone. That's the secret. It's not how it used to be, but that's how it is now. And since things have worked out, it wouldn't be right to be alone."

"I can understand that, Frank."

"She's actually quite excited about it."

"I can imagine."

Frank looked at him. Something like forgiveness appeared in his face. "You know, I used to envy you, Charlie. It always seemed unfair, the way things went along. But I actually feel sorry now. I wish we both could have what we want."

"Maybe we can. You never know."

"I actually feel sorry for you."

Charlie smiled. "It's the power, Frank. It'll wear off."

"I wish you wouldn't say that."

Charlie faced the window. The bay was filled with light. "Good luck, Frank. I mean it."

"Well, thank you, old boy."

"Good luck to you and Julie."

"I want to say the same for you."

"Just close the door on your way out."

* * *

Maju started dying at eleven o'clock. That's when Charlie got the call from the hospital.

"Have you contacted Mrs. Bredesen?" he asked.

"She's away from work, Mr. Bredesen, and there is no answer at home."

He frowned. "I'll come right over."

Charlie took the elevator to the garage. When he had ordered the BMW, he chose a new parking slot between a pillar and a wall so that some asshole couldn't ding the car, and as he walked across the concrete floor, a man got out of a green Riviera three stalls away and came toward him.

"Could I talk to you?" the man said.

Charlie stared at him. There was a blue mouse under the left eye. An adhesive patch was beneath the lower lip, which was puffy and red. A scratch that must have been made by his class ring ran down the left cheek and disappeared into the mouth.

"I know you go out to lunch, and I got here early to wait. It's imperative that we talk."

Charlie felt no anger and this surprised him. Instead there was a hollowness.

"I bear you no malice," Danilow said. "You must understand that. In fact, I'm thankful for what happened. It only verified certain things that I had been deciding, put the seal on them, in a sense." His eyes were moist. "Mr. Bredesen, I want your help. What's more, you need mine."

"I don't buy that."

"Oh, not in any conventional sense. No. Much more vital than that. Because I understand something about you. We have a mission, you and I. There is a way out for both of us."

Parking garages had always bothered Charlie. They were vaults or crypts, where horns echoed and tires squeeled like bats. The air was cold. There was a smell of rust and shadow. Concrete floors, walls, tiny rectangular space and vehicles lined up like coffins. The light was white and pale. The silence, when he was alone, made him feel lost.

"I have an emergency."

"So do we, Mr. Bredesen, and ours is greater." He touched Charlie's arm and Charlie drew back. "I do not mean to harm you. I thought about killing you. I was prepared to maybe kill you. What does it matter? I couldn't really have killed you. I only needed you to take away the suggestion. The hint about survival."

"What hint?"

"Mr. Eisner's."

Charlie leaned against the car. "I don't believe this. It's crazy. I can't believe it."

"Remember, Mr. Bredesen, what killed the cat. And you were more than curious. You were obsessed. Or so it appeared. When it came to breaking into houses."

Charlie turned away.

"I'm grateful to you, don't you understand? In your search for Ruth, you made me find what I had lost. No, not lost. That would be a lie. Set aside. That's better. Conveniently set aside."

Charlie opened the car door and sat down. He reached over and unlocked the passenger door. Danilow sat down beside him.

"Ruth didn't know about the coverup, you see. I was working on a project that had gone bad, that was all. Some women became ill. Then some died. Rather dramatically. We hadn't tested the device thoroughly enough. What with the AIDS scare, it would have made a lot of money. Even for me. It would have been nice for a change to be a little ahead. Ideals don't do anything around the first of the month. But Ruth, she never gave up anything she believed in. She never lost faith in what was true. She made jokes about my wanting to buy things, to be in front a little and not always behind. I laughed too. It was funny, in a way. It wasn't important, but then it seemed so damned important after all. Then she found out. She couldn't bring things together. Me, that is, and the truth. She would have had to join up, don't you see? Either that or tell what she knew. In which case." Danilow waved his hand. "In which case." He put his face in his hand.

"Jesus H. Christ," said Charlie.

"There were only a few of us who knew. The merger would have provided the money to compensate the families, and the old man's name would have been protected. That's all he wanted. He had spent his whole life building that name and didn't want it torn down at the end. He hated all the new rules and regulations. He knew he'd lived too long. But the risk was acceptable, in his opinion. 'If you're going to go forward, you have to take risks.' It was his favorite thing to say. I'd been taking risks politically since Vietnam. So it was all right. It was a cause. Public health and safety. Freedom of choice. What greater things could be imagined. Except truth, maybe."

"You were experimenting," Charlie said.

Danilow looked through the windshield at the concrete wall. "I'm a scientist."

"Scientists don't experiment on human beings."

"No, Mr. Bredesen, you're quite right, of course. But I did not think I was experimenting upon human beings. I actually thought the product was safe. To that point, anyway, I was honest. It was only later, when things went bad, that I began to lie."

Charlie held the steering wheel in both hands. "That's why, then."

"Yes, Mr. Bredesen, as far as I can understand, that's why."

Charlie wasn't looking at him. "I could have stopped it.

"I understand that, Mr. Bredesen."

"I was right there. I just sat there."

Danilow said nothing.

"I could have done something."

"That's why I'm here, Mr. Bredesen."

Charlie turned. Never had he seen a face like this face. The life was gone. There was not even pain. Behind the eyes there was nothing.

"Do you still want to do something for Ruth?"

"What are you talking about?"

"That's what it would be. Symbolically, of course. But at this point, after all, what else can it be? But I think it would be enough. For both of us."

"What do you mean, for both of us? I'm not involved here, you understand? This Safecon thing, it's extraneous to what I did on the bridge."

"I understand."

"It wasn't my fault. I'm not to blame here."

"It's beyond blame, then, isn't it? Something much more important. We're all together, that's what it is. This individuality business, maybe it's a lie just to make money. Maybe there are values, Mr. Bredesen. We all need expiation. We've forgotten what we are, that's all. We've forgotten how to pray."

"I don't know what you're talking about."

"Of course you do. I'm talking about Ruth, you and me."

"I don't know you."

"That's not true."

"I didn't know you."

"That's not true either."

"I have to go now."

"You wouldn't have to do anything actually. But you should be there. Kind of to watch. It would be a moral thing. Something spiritual. It would involve taking sides. That's what we've forgotten, Mr. Bredesen. Taking sides."

Charlie put his head against the steering wheel.

"It's a terrible thing to be impotent. If you won't do this for Ruth, then do it for yourself."

"My mother-in-law is dying. She's at John Muir in Walnut Creek."

"I'll go now," Danilow said.

"No, wait." Charlie put his hand on Danilow's arm. "Tell me."

"I'm going to blow up the lab."

Charlie's mouth opened.

"It's the perfect thing," Danilow said. "The papers. Television. It will topple everything. They won't even know about you. They'll nail me, of course. But then I'll have my stage. That's the way of it. It will make up for things a bit. And you can put something back."

"I can't do it."

"Why not?"

223

"I just can't."

"You won't."

"Maybe I won't."

"Maybe you could have done something on the bridge."

"You sonofabitch."

"Yes, Mr. Bredesen. That's what Ruth said the morning she drove away."

* * *

Her head was pressed into the pillow. On the pillow slip were two patches of wet. They had been put there by the damp cloth the nurse had used. Or by perspiration. Or tears. The old woman's eyes were red when Charlie walked into the room.

He stood at the foot of the bed. There were many things to remember, most of them bad. The tedious roast beef dinners. The lectures about child rearing. The little mannerisms of condescension and superiority. He had never liked Maju and Maju had never liked him. After all, he had been Catholic while they belonged to the First Christian Church. And the more he grew indifferent to religion, the more Maju became concerned about the spiritual well-being of Kelly and David. When her husband, George, died of prostate cancer, she bought jugs of Gallo by the case and proceeded to become a sweet wine alcoholic.

Charlie's heart was in his ears. The nurse was at one side of the bed. The doctor was at the other. The nurse bent over and dabbed the cloth against Maju's forehead and lips. The doctor stepped back and said, "I'm sorry, Mr. Bredesen, but at least she's experiencing no pain."

Charlie walked slowly around to where the doctor had stood. Maju's eyes, as round as marbles, followed him. He stared at her. Her eyes tried to reach up and lay themselves upon his face.

He thought she didn't recognize him. But her eyes left

him and crabbed about the room. When they returned, he saw that she understood everything.

Charlie tried to smile, but with death so imminent, there was nothing to be encouraged about, so he knew he was frowning. He looked down into her face, and an enormous pity welled up in him. He saw himself lying in such a bed, at the finish of the years, confronted by strangers and those he had been unable to love. The lines in the old woman's face were like erosions in a desert.

Charlie wanted to run. He could see that she was terrified to find that she was alone. She had had some other script. She had rehearsed the lines. He could see in her eyes that there were things she wanted to say and that only he was there and she had no one to say them to.

He stepped toward the bed. She shuddered. There were tiny flinchings along her cheeks and throat. He had come to assault her with a final degradation. It was the seal of his boredom at having to watch television with George in the den, the flaring of his nostril wings that he thought she had never observed over the roast beef and the mashed potatoes. He hated her and here he was. At the end, a heartless son-in-law was all she had.

Tears came to her eyes. Standing above her, Charlie watched the little shakings her body made beneath the blankets. "Maju," he said.

At the name she stiffened. He never called her that. He never called her anything really, only, "Hello, how've you been?" and "Well, see you next time." Not giving her a name disallowed her existence, demeaned it. In fact demeaning was a word she had used more than once about him to Marian.

"Maju," Charlie said.

She wanted to brush the tears away. She was a lump of flesh in which life whimpered out. He took the cloth from the nurse and wiped her eyes.

225

She opened her mouth. Her lips were corrugated paper. They formed a circle and she wheezed.

"She's very weak," the doctor said.

Charlie turned to him. "Please don't say anything else."

In the silence he could hear the air draw across her lungs. That death should be so clumsy, so embarrassing, both for the living and the dying, was too much. He found himself hating Marian for having abandoned them.

He took her hand. She had not the strength to take his. He held her fingers and looked away. There were machines beside the bed, instruments against the wall. There was the smell of antiseptic. He could hear the nurse's uniform when she moved.

He remembered being alone on the river in Montana. He was alone now. But on the river there was something grand. It was made up of the water, the trees, the mountains and sky. He stood in the center alone, and that was as it should be and quite natural. But here, with his own kind, there was something sinister, something terrible. Everything shrank away, leaving only death. At the center was nothing.

He felt a motion in his hand. He looked at Maju. She was trying to speak. A pulse moved across her lips. He bent to listen and heard a tiny rush of breath.

The old woman's eyes were shining. There was darkness all around, and the eyes were burning bright. She would hold back the darkness. Momentarily she would grasp this reason to live. It was in the eyes. And the eyes were burning upon his face.

Charlie understood. He straightened but felt the fingers close in his hand. With her last strength she raised her head from the pillow. The pulse quickened across her lips. Her body trembled.

"No, Maju," he said.

The doctor bent over her, trying to hold her down. The

eyes were fires in Charlie's brain. She had surrendered everything, the bitterness, the hate. There would be no one else. Charlie was what she had. And if that was all, then it was enough. Charlie was enough for her to say what she would say.

He tried to pull away but he felt her nails in the palm of his hand. Then she spoke. One word. It took all of her life.

She fell back and the fingers collapsed. He put the hand upon the bed. The doctor fussed a bit. Charlie was weeping.

"What does it mean?" the doctor said.

"Forgive," Charlie said. He felt it rising in his heart. "That's all she could say."

"That's odd," the doctor replied. "I could have sworn it was, 'Forget.'"

* * *

Charlie pushed the front door open and entered the house. He went into the living room, the family room. Then he walked into the kitchen. Marian was sitting at the kitchen table, a drink in her hand.

"Don't tell me," she said. "Don't say the words."

He sat down. "Where are the kids?"

"David's upstairs. Kelly had some practice or other."

Charlie looked at her. "Does David know?"

"No," she said.

"How did you find out?":

"The hospital got me. You had just left."

"They were trying to get you all morning."

"Well, they got me." She began to cry.

"Sorry," Charlie said.

"I don't want you to be sorry."

"What does that mean?"

"I don't know." She swallowed from the drink. "You can be sorry if you want to. Be my guest. Be sorry. You don't have to look at me like that. You can be sorry without looking that

227

way."

"How am I looking?"

"That way."

Charlie went to the refrigerator and filled a glass with water. He pushed the lever for the ice cubes, came back to the table and sat down.

"Did she say anything?" Marian asked.

"No."

"Nothing?"

He shook his head.

"I feel awful."

"You ought to."

"You don't have to say that. No, say it. You should say it." She swallowed from the drink. "Was there any. . .? Did she. . .?"

"The doctor said no."

"But did you see anything?"

"No," he said.

"Are you lying?"

"You're drunk. When did you start getting drunk?"

"A long time ago."

"Too long ago."

"Don't get smart, buster."

Charlie drank some water. "What a way to talk."

"How do you talk? Tell me. I don't know anything about how to talk. When dad died, it wasn't the same. What do you say now?"

"I don't know what to say."

"I know what to say, but I can't say it."

"Say what you want to say."

"I can't." Her eyes were filling.

"Say it."

"I can't, Charlie."

"Go on."

"I'm sorry. I'm so sorry."

"For the way I was looking?"

"And everything."

"About your mother."

"I'm sorry you didn't like her."

"I liked her."

"You never liked her."

"Today, I liked her."

"What happened?"

"I liked her."

He took the drink out of her hand and set it on the table.

"The kids are going to need you. Particularly Kelly."

She nodded and blew her nose. "I'm sorry."

"We're saying that a lot."

"What do you mean?"

"We've said I'm sorry a half dozen times."

"We're pretty sorry people." She tried to flash a smile.

"Hey."

"Sorry."

She looked at the floor. He wrapped his fingers around the glass and moved it back and forth on the table.

"Are you going to call Henderson's?" Henderson's had buried George.

"I called after I talked to the hospital. They're taking care of things. I'll go over tomorrow."

He nodded.

"How did she look?" Marian asked.

"Worn out," Charlie said.

She put her hand over her eyes. "You start to think of the things you could have said."

"Or done."

She looked at him. "You didn't have to say that."

"It's a waste of time to think like that. It could never be enough. So what's the point?"

"Are you mad?"

"Why?"

"You seem mad."

"I'm not mad. I was, but I'm not."

"What do you mean?"

"I'm relieved. Please don't drink anymore."

She put the glass down.

"Did you find out something?"

"Yes."

Her eyes widened. "I'm sorry, Charlie. It's all so foolish and I'm so sorry."

"What are you talking about?"

"It doesn't mean a goddamn thing. It never did."

"How did you find out?"

"What?"

"I thought you wanted me to be president." He looked at her eyes. "What are you talking about?"

"Nothing."

He took the glass out of her hand. "You're talking about nothing."

"Yes. Nothing. What happened," she waved her hand, "at work?"

"What's so foolish, Marian?"

"The whole thing. Everything. Life."

"Your mother's death?"

"What? No, of course not."

"We were talking about that, weren't we?"

"I don't have either one of my parents now. Do you know what a strange feeling it is to have both your parents gone?"

Charlie watched her.

"It's like floating on a raft way out at sea." She lifted the drink. "Way out at sea. It's better for her, I guess. I couldn't tell what was going on in her mind lately. It felt very strange not to know."

230

"Fuck," Charlie said.

"What?" Her lips were trembling.

"You heard me."

He got up and went to the sink. He emptied the glass. Then he refilled it and pushed the lever for cubes. He came back and stood over her.

"Sit down, Charlie."

"I'd rather stand."

"Please sit down."

He stepped to the chair but remained standing. "It must be a terrible kind of guilt."

"Shut up!"

"On the day your mother died. I offer it only as an observation. I wouldn't want to be in that place."

"You sonofabitch."

"No. No. That's not fair. It must be terrible. I'm on your side. What a thing to have to live with."

"Shut up! Shut up!"

He sat down.

"I'm not going to be president of the new company, you know. It's all tumbled over. What's more I don't care. But I liked your mother today. And I never thought I would. That's something. For a generally fucked day, that is. Yet, I'm not mad. I should be, though, shouldn't I? But I'm not. I don't know why. It's my duty to be mad. I'm not. Believe me, it's a relief. It's kind of fair in a way. When the wind goes out of the sails, it might as well all go."

"What do you mean by that?"

"Time to get out and run?"

"What are you saying?"

"I really don't know. Call it a hunch."

"All right, so I'm feeling guilty about Mother. If you want to know the truth, I feel damned guilty about everything. I wish it hadn't happened. None of it. Fix me a drink, will you?"

"I don't want to fix you a drink."

"Will you fix me a goddamn drink? Can't you let me have a little goddamn dignity?"

He went to the sink and returned with the Canadian Club. He set it on the table.

"I don't want to leave you," she said.

Charlie sat down.

"It didn't mean anything like that."

"What did it mean?"

"Nothing. Absolutely nothing." She poured the bourbon into the glass.

"And that's why?"

"Maybe that is why. Maybe that's why everything. It doesn't mean anything. And so that's why. Why is it for you?"

"What are you talking about?"

"I'm talking about why you do what you do."

Charlie put his hand flat down on the table and looked at each of the fingers.

"Didn't you think I knew all this time you've been dicking around?"

Charlie looked at her. "I supposed you didn't."

She laughed."This is the age of sattelite television and cellular phones. Everybody knows everything. So it doesn't matter, does it?"

"It doesn't matter?"

"Well, it does and it doesn't. Maybe it just can't matter. Not anymore anyway."

A feeling came over him. It was unfamiliar. He was used to the irony, the cynicism and indifference. He could smell bullshit a mile away. He had invested most of his adult life learning to smell it. But he had made mistakes of late, bad mistakes. There was something he had forgotten to bring along through the years. It wasn't innocence or youth. It just

232

hadn't gone along for the ride, that's all. And he looked at Marian and missed it, whatever it was.

"I found out about that last one," she said. "That secretary person or whatever she is, at work."

Charlie said nothing.

"It isn't all that interesting anyway, if you ask me. It's over quick and you sweat and don't walk away with anything. It's all left behind, if you know what I mean. Maybe it's boredom. Is it boredom, Charlie?"

"I don't know what it is," he said. They were prizefighters talking over old bouts. "I don't think I was bored with you."

"No, not that kind of boredom. Just boredom."

"Maybe it's some of that."

"I think maybe it is. There's too much to do, but not enough to do, not really. Everything's in pieces. All our lives are made up of these pieces. Something here, something there. It's like we live in a hundred places but no place all at once."

Charlie looked over her shoulder at the drainboard, where the afternoon light was making the shadow of the leaves move.

"Charlie, I don't want a divorce. That's not in your mind, is it?"

He didn't say anything.

"I don't want another man. In spite of anything, I never did. It makes it all stupid, doesn't it?"

"Maybe not stupid."

"Well, thank you for that. I know I'm not stupid. Half of the people in this state have been divorced. Three-fourths of the married men and half of the married women sleep around."

"Where did you hear that?"

"I read it in a magazine."

"That's something."

"It's a way of life. You almost feel out of it if you don't screw somebody else."

"Is that how you felt?"

"No. Of course not."

"Then what?"

"What did you feel?"

"Alone," he said.

"Don't I satisfy you, Charlie?"

"Of course you do. And me?"

"Yes."

"We're right back where we started."

"Maybe it's human nature."

"I don't think so."

"There's something about us."

"I don't think it's that either."

She drank from the glass. He did not try to stop her. "I know I need a place." She patted the table. "Something that's there. That's just there. I feel like I'm in a wind tunnel most of the time. They keep reinventing the wheel every few years. I'm beginning to think it was better the way it was."

"I know what you mean."

"You're the best I know. I haven't done much, Charlie. You have to believe that. It doesn't even have to do with you and me. Really. I like our life together. I really do. We have a good thing, don't you think? There's confusion maybe, but that's not our fault. It's all that way. It's in the air or something. I don't want a divorce, Charlie. I really don't." She fixed her eyes on his. "Do you?"

"I don't know."

She began to cry. He went to the drainboard and returned with the box of Kleenex.

"Does it hurt?" she asked.

"Yes."

"It hurts me too. There's so much hurt."

"Maybe we should stop talking about it."

"I'm glad you were with Mother, Charlie. I'm such a shit."

"Don't say that."

"A goddamn shit."

"Cut it out."

"My own mother. Can you beat it? I let her down. I let my own mother down for a piece of ass. What a shit."

Charlie looked at her.

"Drive me over to Henderson's?"

"You were going tomorrow."

"I'm a fucking coward, that's all. I should go now. I can at least get that back. Just drive me over, will you? I want to see her."

"You're in no condition."

"I want to see her, goddamnit. C'mon."

"No," he said.

"What?"

"No. I won't drive you. If you want to go, get Dave to do it."

"Charlie!"

He stood up. "Listen, I don't want to deal with any more of this right now. I don't want to go to Henderson's and have you rub out whatever I had with your mother today. I want it that way, with just the memory of it."

"Wait out in the goddamn car then."

"You don't understand."

"So I am stupid."

"Cut it out."

"Drop me off and come back later."

"I don't trust you."

"What the hell's that supposed to mean?"

"Call it a hunch."

"You and your fucking hunches."

"All the years between your mother and me you were there. Today is just going to stay today."

"You bastard."

She struggled to stand but slipped and plopped down in the chair. Kelly came into the room. "Mom," she cried. "What's wrong?"

"Maju died, Sweetheart, and your father here won't drive me to the funeral home."

Charlie looked at his daughter. She took the whole scene in at a glance. He could see her trying to process it. She wanted to cry. Her eyes were full ,but she was as stiff as a post. She looked at Marian and then at him. "I hate you!" she screamed. "I hate you both!" Then she burst into tears.

Without another word Charlie left the room.

* * *

The motel was in Lafayette, a few miles up the road toward the Caldecott. You came off the freeway and there were pine trees. You parked around back and the wind was high in the needles of the pines. There were shadows under the lights. It felt like something around Mendocino or Ft. Bragg.

He had been talking to himself all the way from Walnut Creek, but he could remember nothing of the conversation. It was pleasant in the darkness beneath the trees. There is no time in the parking stalls of motels. You can sit there forever and history will never happen.

He climbed the stairs to the second floor and went down a narrow hallway. He stopped and waited. Then he put his fingers against the door.

"Jesus Christ," Vivian said when he entered the room.

"That bad, huh?"

"You look awful."

"I went for a run in the park."

"In your houndstooth?"

"I wanted to run. I was going to clean up. I didn't want to go back home. Maybe I could use your shower?" He held up a shopping bag. "I have some clean stuff."

"Of course, baby. But what is it?"

While he got undressed he told her about the day. He didn't tell her about Danilow.

"We're both having bad luck," she said.

"Has something else happened?"

"I drove by the place after work. Garbage was dumped all over the lawn again. I had to stop and clean it up."

"Don't go there," he said.

"How can I sell the place with a mess like that in the front yard? I have to go there."

"I don't want you to go anymore unless someone's along."

"All right. I need to get a few things."

"I'll drive you over."

"You look mighty good to me."

"I'd like to sleep here tonight."

"You got it," she said.

He climbed into the shower. It was very satisfactory. He set the water as hot as he could stand it. He held his head under the water for a long time.

"Hungry?" she asked, watching him towel off.

"Yes."

"I can fix you a sandwich. I have some beer."

"That's fine," he said.

It was one of those kitchenettes with a tiny refrigerator and a small, rectangular stove. He put on the sneakers, jeans and sweatshirt and opened a beer.

"There'll be a sign on the lawn tomorrow," she said. "I expect that will make the nigger haters happy. They'll leave the place alone and I'll get that apartment."

"Good," he said, kissing her on the neck. "The sooner

you're out of there the better."

"But it pisses me."

"Yeah, I know."

"You don't know. But it still pisses me."

"Still got the corner on suffering, I see."

"The market share, honey. The market share."

He went to the kitchen window and looked out. He could see a piece of the freeway and the lights of the houses in the hills beyond.

"I still like you a whole lot, no matter what."

"My white-ass honkey sonofabitch."

"I love it."

"You're not."

"Sure I am."

"No. You're just white. White, that's all. And I'm black. That's all."

"That's just right."

"That's good enough, isn't it?"

"Better. It's just better."

"Charlie?"

"What?"

She spread the mayonnaisse over the salami. "Nothing. I'm sorry you're not going to be president."

"I'm not sorry."

"What will you do?"

"I don't know."

"Does it matter?"

He thought about it a moment. "No," he said.

They sat down at the formica table and drank the beer. He bit into the sandwich.

"Good," he said.

"Do you want another?"

"Sure."

She got up and unwrapped the bread. "Charlie?"

"Yes?"

"Things are different now, aren't they?"

"What do you mean?"

"You know what I mean."

He chewed the sandwich and watched her.

"I'm thinking of leaving my job, Charlie."

"What happened?"

"Nothing happened. I'm just not doing anything. I'm not doing enough. I've been thinking about it awhile. I was thinking about it before I met you. This thing with the house. And all I'm doing is servicing a bunch of white-ass kids so they can get into the college of their choice." She brought the fresh sandwich and set it down before him. "Another beer?"

"Sure."

"Identity crisis, home boy. I was so damned glad to get out of L.A. I thought the job here meant something had changed. But there are only a handful of black kids in the entire district. So who am I kidding? You can take the nigger out of the ghetto. You dig? Ruth had it right. She was down there in the trenches. I'm just a pussy. A damned black pussy. When she died, I knew just how afraid I had always been. Isn't that the shits?"

"Maybe you're being too hard on yourself."

"Maybe I'm not being hard enough. These bastards with their goddamn phone calls and their tampax on my lawn. I want to kick their fucking ass and here I am running again."

"You have to save your life, for chrissake. That's all you're doing right now. You're just saving your life."

"But things are different, Charlie."

"You mean about me."

"Different. Me. You."

"You mean us."

"Us. There is no us, remember? There's you, me, but no us."

"Vivian."

"I'm sorry. I'm mad. There's us. A very nice us. I'm so glad there's us. Maybe I'm just afraid of us."

He took her hand.

"That's my problem, you know. I've always stayed close to myself. You have to, you know. Ruth was the only one." Her lips trembled. "Maybe I shouldn't worry all the time about safe. Safe. Safe. Maybe we should do something and fuck safe. And I'm thinking lately I really want to do something. If I'm saving my life, it's got to be for something that counts. I'm holed up in this goddamn motel like a scared black rabbit. But rabbits have teeth, you know. Sharp teeth. All they have to do is turn and bite."

"What would you do?"

"Give all those honky bastards something really to get nervous about."

Charlie went to the sink. He looked out the window at the edge of the freeway and the hills beyond.

"What is it, honey?"

"I don't know. It's all happened so fast."

"You mean us?"

"No. No. Well, that too. But everything. You go along and then something happens and everything changes. Not just one thing. Everything. It makes you think. Why should one thing be so fucking important?" He turned to face her. "What if I had gotten out of the car that morning. If I had run over to her and pulled her back. Taken her someplace and talked. Anything. But I just sat there. I couldn't get around so I just sat there." He came back to the table. "It was my fault, Viv. I could have saved Ruth and I didn't. It was my fault. I've been thinking about it and I've decided."

"Charlie."

"No. No. That's it. That's just it."

"Charlie, you can't think that way."

"Why do you think the way you do?"

"It's not the same. You had no way of knowing."

"People don't get out of cars in the middle of the Bay Bridge and walk over to the side."

"You're not responsible."

"I am."

"It's not true. Why are you doing this? I thought you were through with this."

"I stuck my tongue out at her."

"Jesus, Charlie."

"Your best friend. I'm responsible. That's it. You were talking about protecting yourself. Well, check out yours truly. Sit in the car and watch. Beat my meat at the office. Look out the window and daydream. Nice and safe. So what am I saving myself for?" He slapped his chest. "Answer me that. What's good ol' Charlie Bredesen worth saving for?"

She put a hand against his.

"How about making love with a nigger?"

He grinned. "That's something worth living for."

"Well, you got the job as long as you want it."

"A labor of love."

She looked at him. "OK, honey."

They sat for awhile. There was too much to think about but it didn't matter. He liked being there and wanting her and not doing anything about it. The tiny refrigerator came on. He waited a while. Then he took her hand.

"Let's go get that stuff," he said.

They went down the stairs and out into the lot. It was cooler now, the wind still high in the needles of the pines. The wind made that sound as it came through the needles, like something sighing. It always made him look up.

They walked to the BMW. A dirty white van was parked next to it. When he put the key into the lock, the side door of the van slammed open and three men jumped out. The men wore grocery bags over their heads. They came around the car from both ends, and one of the grocery bags said, "Nigger." The bag was wearing a 49er sweatshirt.

Charlie squared himself. Another grocery bag with a white tee-shirt came from the front of the car and kicked Charlie in the stomach. Charlie doubled over and fell. His face struck the concrete tire guard.

Vivian screamed. The 49er grocery bag hit her hard. Charlie heard something crack and tried to turn his head. His wind was gone and he couldn't breathe, but he saw blood coming from Vivian's mouth and nose. Even in the light of the parking lot he was startled to see how red her blood was.

The other grocery bag and the tee-shirt bag rolled Charlie over and tied his hands behind him with bailing twine. They lifted him. The pain in his stomach was so severe that he could not stand. They leaned him against the BMW. Charlie saw the 49er bag stuff something into Vivian's mouth and tie it there with a dishcloth. Then the 49er bag took something out of his pocket and shoved it into Charlie's mouth. He tied it off with a dishcloth. Charlie wanted to throw up. The tee-shirt bag hit him in the kidney. He doubled over again, biting into the bar of soap. He wouldn't swallow. But he had to swallow. The two grocery bags picked him up and threw him into the van. Vivian was lying there crying in a puddle of blood.

The three grocery bags sat on the floor of the van, and somebody else began driving. The grocery bags did not talk. Charlie's mouth was on fire. Something was wrong with one of his ankles. The car went up onto the freeway and began to go very fast.

"Slow down," one of the grocery bags said. "We don't need a fucking ticket." Then the grocery bags tied Charlie's feet together.

Charlie put his head against the floor of the van.

Sometimes the lights from the freeway came through the windows and onto the floor. He could see Vivian's face. Her eyes were very wide and unblinking and they stared straight at him.

After awhile the van left the freeway. Charlie still heard traffic. They had not gone out into the country as he had feared, so maybe the bags were going to finish with them and then drop them on the street somewhere. The van made a turn, went some distance and stopped.

The driver came around the side of the van and the door opened. Now the driver was wearing a bag too. He helped the 49er bag lift Vivian out of the van. They pushed her to the ground. Then they threw Charlie out. He could see they had tied Vivian's ankles.

They were on a paved area of some kind. It was dark and there were trees. Lights dripped through the branches. He rolled over onto his back and lifted his head. He could see cars moving through the trees along a street, but the street was a city block away. Then he knew where he was.

The 49er bag took a heavy rope out of the van. It had a loop at one end and a thick knot. When Vivian saw the rope, she commenced to roll over and over, but the bag who had been driving grabbed her by the hair and slammed her against the van. Charlie shouted through the dishcloth but nothing happened. He tried to push himself against the legs, but the tee-shirt bag kicked him in the stomach and all the wind went out of him.

Charlie lay on his side and watched as the 49er bag threw the loose end of the rope over the branch of an oak tree. The other bags dragged Vivian to the tree and lifted her head. Then the bag who had kicked him propped Charlie up against the trunk of the tree.

The bag who had been driving put the rope around Vivian's head. She stared at Charlie. All the time she kept

243

staring at him. The bags took the free end of the rope and went back with it. Vivian came off the ground and turned in circles, kicking. Charlie shut his eyes. He kept them shut. He screamed through the dishcloth. He pushed his head against the corrugations of the tree until the blood came. Then the van started and drove away.

Charlie's eyes were closed. He sat against the trunk of the tree. He moved his wrists. It was easier to move them. He could get them free. But he sat there. Tears ran down his face into the dishcloth. He wanted to do something. So he opened his eyes.

He did not move his wrists. He cried. He sat a long time crying with his eyes open. Finally, three hundred yards away, the last train of the evening pulled into the BART station.

* * *

"Spread out that newspaper."

Charlie opened the paper and placed it on the workbench. Danilow went to the back of the garage and returned with a three foot square plank and a plastic bucket.

"Get that bag of fertilizer there by the rake, will you?"

"Fertilizer?" Charlie said.

"We're going to blow the shit out of the place, aren't we, Mr. Bredesen? Put a couple handfuls on the board and rub the particles to powder with that wooden block. Pile it up until I ask you to stop. Make a fine powder now. About the consistency of flour."

Charlie began crushing the fertilizer. He watched as Danilow drilled a hole halfway down the length of a galvanized pipe. The pipe was about the length of his forearm and two inches in diameter. There was a cap screwed on one end.

"Do you know what we're making?"

"I have no idea," said Charlie.

"Welcome to the world of terrorism. Only we're not

244

terrorists, are we?" He finished with the hole and put the drill back on the wall above the bench. "We're building a pipe bomb. With an incendiary variation."

Danilow poured a cup of kerosene into the bucket and then measured in one cup after another of the powdered fertilizer. He stirred the bucket with a wooden dowel.

"I don't get it," Charlie said.

"Basic chemistry," Danilow said. "About sixteen parts powder to one part fuel oil. We make enough to fill the pipe. Loosely, of course. If we pack it too tight, it will be dangerous."

When he filled the pipe, Danilow screwed on the other cap and set the pipe on the counter.

"So you decided."

"Yes," said Charlie.

"Isn't it strange how we rationalize everything? Have you figured out why you're really here, Mr. Bredesen?"

Charlie looked at the pipe lying on the bench.

"I almost feel we should talk about it. Justification makes people strong."

"Aren't we strong enough?" Charlie said.

"Yes. I suppose we are."

"I don't know what else there is to talk about."

"I suppose nothing. But I do want to say something anyway. I want to say I'm truly ashamed. It's a terrible thing to be ashamed, Mr. Bredesen. It's not like being sorry. I'm ashamed of myself." He put his hand on the pipe. "It doesn't make any difference. It's a terrible think to look back. Regret is a terrible thing. And shame is a terrible justification. So I will think there is something more worthy than shame."

He opened a small cardboard box and removed a cylindrical object about the size of his little finger. Two wires were attached to the object.

"This is the blasting cap, Mr. Bredesen. I'll push the cap

into the hole until only the wires are exposed. Then I'll plug the hole with putty." He reached into the paper bag and removed a six volt battery and a small alarm clock. "I've drilled a hole through the crystal and set in a screw. The head of the screw is just high enough so that when the minute hand makes contact, the circuit will close and the bomb will dentonate. I'll attach the wire and wind the clock just before I leave the building.

"That's all there is to it?"

"That's all for the bomb, Mr. Bredesen. Now for the incendiary surprise. Hand me that can of gasoline."

Danilow filled two cheap wine bottles with the gasoline and screwed on the caps. He taped the bottles to the galvanized pipe and covered the end of the pipe with the hollowed out end of a loaf of French bread.

"I'll tell the security gaurd I'm having a little celebration. When the bomb goes off, it will throw the gasoline everywhere. A nice pyrotechnic display."

Charlie stepped back.

"It is frightening, isn't it?"

"What about the people?"

"No people, Mr. Bredesen. The lab is a separate building, quite apart from anything else. Very sound walls. All the destruction will be confined to the interior. But the roof will lift. The energy has to go somewhere, after all." He put everything into the bag. "I think we're ready. Would you like to carry it?"

"Yes," Charlie said.

He picked up the bag. The palms of his hands were wet and stuck to the paper. They went outside and Danilow locked the garage.

"Not much point to this, I suppose."

Charlie looked at him.

"We'll take your car, Mr. Bredesen."

246

They got into the BMW and Danilow directed him to the street in Concord where the plant was located. Charlie held his hands on the wheel and stared straight ahead. Danilow looked out the side window. The bag was on the seat between them.

When they got to the plant, Charlie switched off the engine.

"We'll say goodbye here, Mr. Bredesen."

Charlie put his arms around the bag. A moment passed. Then Charlie lifted the bag and handed it to Danilow.

"You're smiling, Mr. Bredesen."

"I was thinking of my daughter," Charlie said.

Danilow opened the door. "You should go now."

"I'll wait," Charlie said.

"Goodbye, then."

"Goodbye."

Danilow walked across the street. He stopped at a tiny building next to a large gate. He tapped on a window. A door opened in the building. Danilow disappeared.

Charlie waited. Fifteen minutes passed. Then he heard a muffled "whump" and then a secondary, louder roar. A spear of flame shot into the air. A siren went off. Charlie started the BMW and drove away.

The next day there was a story in the paper and a picture of Abe Danilow and old man Eisner. There was a picture of Vivian too, but he did not read about her.

He went to the BMW dealer and sold the car. He took a cab to the bank and cashed out a small certificate of deposit and a personal savings account. He had the money in one hundred dollar bills in a pouch tied around his waist.

Then Charlie started running. He ran down Ygnacio. That would take him to the outskirts of town and the valley beyond. He wore his tennis shoes and grey sweats.

It was an easy pace, one he could keep up indefinitely. He

passed the houses, the buildings and stoplights. He noticed that it was a beautiful day. He smiled.

Flat footed, his knees bent, his arms swinging loosely, Charlie Bredesen ran right out of his life.